Underwater Wasteland

"Have faith, Comrade Camellion, God will protect you."

That's what the Soviet scientist had said. God? Down here at the bottom of the ocean in this world of polychrome steel? The Death Merchant looked through the transparent dome to the fifty feet of water above his head; the sodium-vapor lights making the icy water glow grotesquely. From the sides of the cubical the sea glared at him, waiting . . . waiting to fill his lungs with pressing, frigid death.

It was one helluva mission, down here in this underwater wasteland. The domes were all that was keeping the furious Arctic waters from flooding in and ending his career in one big splash. The Death Merchant glanced up at the blue concave ceiling and saw a crack widening. "Not yet, you son of a bitch. I've still gotta earn my five hundred grand."

But how the hell would he make it to the lockout chamber of the sub and still stay alive? The Death Merchant decided to make a go at it. He had nothing to lose but his life!

The Death Merchant Series:

#17

DEATH MERCHANT
THE ZEMLYA EXPEDITION
by Joseph Rosenberger

PINNACLE BOOKS   NEW YORK CITY

DEATH MERCHANT: THE ZEMLYA EXPEDITION

Copyright © 1976 by Pinnacle Books, Inc.

An original Pinnacle Books edition, published for the first time anywhere.

ISBN: 0-523-00880-5

First printing, July 1976

Cover illustration by Dean Cate

Printed in the United States of America

PINNACLE BOOKS, INC.
275 Madison Avenue
New York, N.Y. 10016

This book is dedicated
to
Michael Holtz
&
Terri Holtz
USAF

"The nation that first learns to understand the oceans will control them, and the nation that controls the seas will rule the world."

Professor G. V. Petrovich
Lenin Institute

"Knowledge of the oceans is more than a matter of curiosity. Our very survival in the future may depend on it."

John F. Kennedy

THE ZEMLYA EXPEDITION

Chapter One

If skepticism is the last refuge of the idealist, Richard J. Camellion had to be the most pessimistic human being on board the *Mikhail Lomonosov*—the Russian oceanographic vessel that had just left the harbor at Stryelka, the only city on the third island of Severnaya Zemlya. There was another bitter certainty, one that stabbed the Death Merchant with invisible ice picks of loneliness: he had to be the only American within hundreds of miles. His nearest countrymen were the U.S. Navy men on board the *Albacore*, the nuclear submarine waiting about 125 nautical miles north—assuming that all had gone well. Assuming that the Gf mechanism on the sub functioned at peak efficiency and prevented the boat from being spotted by Soviet Asdic and other devices which could detect submerged underwater craft. To make matters worse, it was midwinter in this isolated part of the Soviet world. The temperature hovered at forty-two degrees below zero Fahrenheit, and the sun slept below the horizon—common phenomena for areas well within the Arctic Circle.

The Death Merchant was disgusted. Everything that could have gone wrong with the mission had gone wrong, and he found it fantastic that he should have gotten even this far—actually on board the *Mikhail Lomonosov!* Even a man of his diverse and unique talents should have been dead a week ago.

Dressed in a Russian Kelotex-and-nylon wind-resistant parka, heavy pants of similar material, and white cold-weather boots, he waited impatiently in the number four cargo hold of the Soviet vessel, snuggled down between two crates of machinery. His present plan was a ridiculous long shot, but it was the only chance he had; and if the plan succeeded he might get to Zemlya II.

Time trickled by, the long minutes knotting them-

1

selves into cords of boring hours. Cramped, hungry, and thirsty, Camellion waited, sizing up each Russian sailor or officer who came into the cargo hold. Damn it, either they were too short or too tall, too fat or too thin, or else they had some facial characteristic too complicated for him to duplicate with the small makeup kit he carried.

After some four hours, Camellion did see one man who would have been an almost perfect subject. The man was just about his own height and build, and his facial characteristics, on the FBI scale of identification, were similar to Camellion's: long-shaped head, oblong face, straight hairline, normal-fold eyelids, thin lips, straight nose, close ears, and normal chin. Only the man's eyebrows differed from the Death Merchant's. Richard's eyebrows were arched. The Russian's were of a type known as "raised ends."

Not that it made a damn bit of difference! Richard couldn't kill him, anyway. Four other Russians were with the man, who was an ordinary seaman. Sending them off to deathland wouldn't have been a problem. Richard could have iced all five within seconds, using his silenced 9mm Browning pistol. He didn't do it because the KGB knew he had reached Severnaya Zemlya. For over a week they had been tearing the island apart in their efforts to find him, although it was very unlikely that they suspected he had slipped aboard the *Mikhail Lomonosov*. But they sure as hell would if four men disappeared from the vessel. He could impersonate one man, but not four!

Camellion thought of what Teddy Roosevelt had once said: "Do what you can, with what you have, where you are." Uh huh! Good advice! Only Roosevelt had never been alone on a Russian ship, trying to get to an undersea city on a mission for the National Security Agency (NSA) of the United States Government!

I might as well be halfway to the planet Mars! Camellion continued to wait. He became alive with awareness when he heard the lockwheel turning on the aft bulkhead door. He tensed and waited hearing the door swing open, then swing shut when the man closed it. Whoever it was, the sailor was whistling a Russian folk tune, and Camellion could tell from the drift of the sound that the man was walking down the center of the hold. There were no other sounds, only the creaking of ropes and straps holding the cargo in place.

The Death Merchant waited until the man had passed the crates he was hiding behind; then he reared up and looked out after the man who had a clip board in his hand and was taking inventory of cargo at the forward end of the hold. This time Lady Luck—the pretty slut—was with Camellion. For the man was the same seaman who had previously been in the hold in the company of four other men. It would be so easy to pop him off with a 9mm Hi Power Browning slug. Camellion couldn't; his own personal code of ethics would not permit him to gun down a defenseless opponent. When an enemy was trying to kill you, that was a different matter—then you used the most expedient method available to put him to sleep forever.

As silently as a drifting shadow in some forgotten grave yard, Camellion crept out from between the crates and, his hands held out in a goju-ryu karate attack position, moved toward the Russian, whose back was turned to him. He wasn't more than eight feet from the unsuspecting man when all his luck went bad! With a slight creaking, the aft bulkhead door swung open and Maxim Geraskin stepped into the hold. Yuri Drozdov followed him.

At the sight of the Death Merchant creeping up on Valentin Prisk, the two Russians froze for a split second, then swung into action. Geraskin's hand dived beneath his padded coat for a pistol. Unarmed, Drozdov advanced with a strap tightener used to secure the metal straps holding the cargo in place.

Valentin Prisk had also been alerted by the sound of the bulkhead door opening. He swung around, saw the Death Merchant, pulled up short, and did what he thought was best: he threw the fiberboard clipboard at Camellion, who instantly did what he considered his best move. Knowing from experience that the two men who had just entered were more dangerous, he executed a high-flying, double-legged, thunder kick, the pile-driver of savate. His body practically horizontal, Camellion

3

torpedoed across the hold, the thick soles of his boots smashing with such force into Maxim Geraskin's mid-section that the man was knocked six feet back against the metal wall. The Death Merchant twisted his body and jumped erect as Geraskin cried out in pain, dropped his Makarov automatic, and sagged to the floor, gasping loudly.

Yuri Drozdov, with a lightning-quick motion, swung the strap tightener at Camellion's head. As fast as the Russian was the Death Merchant still had the edge by half a blink. All in one motion, Richard dodged the strap tightener, bunched the fingers of his right hand into a deadly *nukite* spear, and stabbed Drozdov directly in the Adam's apple with all his might. His windpipe crushed, Yuri Drozdov began choking to death. He died almost as quickly as Valentin Prisk was able to swing in on the Death Merchant. Prisk was not armed with a pistol, but he had taken an awl from his coat pocket and was using it as a dagger. He had used the awl to punch small holes in the thin wood of some crates, in order to tag them properly. Now he intended to put a nice deep hole in the Death Merchant. In all the world, he couldn't have chosen a more dangerous adversary.

Just as Prisk swung the awl downward, Maxim Geraskin, on his knees to the right of Camellion, reached for the Makarov pistol lying on the floor. Although he had received the full power of the Death Merchant's thunder kick, the blow had only knocked the wind out of him. His thick coat had absorbed most of the force and saved him from serious injury.

Camellion kicked the Makarov to one side and twisted around in time to avoid the four-inch blade of the descending awl. Grabbing Prisk by the wrist, he savagely twisted the man's arm outward and gave him a powerful *hiraken* blow between the eyes. He couldn't kill the man, not yet. He had to hear him speak in order to know if he could duplicate his voice. Stunned, Prisk began to wilt, sinking to his knees, his brain bruised with a big blackness.

In the meanwhile the Death Merchant turned his attention to Maxim Geraskin, who had managed to get to his feet and was rushing Camellion, his arms raised

4

high. A big man, Geraskin was noted for his strength and for his ability as a weight-lifter. His plan was to grab Camellion in a bear hug and crush him into unconsciousness. Then Geraskin made the biggest mistake of his life. He charged straight at the Death Merchant like a wild bull. Richard waited until the final moment, then presented the big Russian with the surprise of his life. Camellion powed him with a *sokuto geri,* a sword foot kick to the pit of the stomach. With a loud cry of agony, Geraskin automatically doubled over. As he bent over, Geraskin presented his head to Camellion, who instantly took advantage of the golden opportunity. He stepped slightly to one side and threw his right arm around the man's neck, his forearm tight against the Russian's throat, forcing Geraskin's head to lay heavily against his right side.

The Death Merchant's next move was fatal to Maxim Geraskin. Taking a deep breath, Richard jumped several feet into the air. To insure a tight hold, he locked the fingers of his right hand with the fingers of his left hand. At the same time, he threw his body forcefully to the left. Unprepared for the sudden movement, Geraskin's body tried to comply with the sideways motion, but the strain was too much for the top vertebrae of his spine. They snapped like an extra-dry twig. His neck broken, Geraskin sagged in death. Camellion released the corpse and spun toward Valentin Prisk, who had halfway shaken the mud from his mind and, still on his knees, was trying to reach the Makarov pistol six feet away. Before the dazed Russian knew what was happening, Camellion dropped behind him and grabbed him around the throat in an unbreakable rear strangle hold, his right forearm against the Russian's Adam's apple, his left elbow boring into Prisk's left shoulder, his left hand on the back of the man's head, his right hand grasping the biceps of his left arm.

"If you as much as sneeze, I'll break your neck!" Camellion hissed in perfect Russian. "Tell me your name and rank!"

"Who are you, the *Amerikanski* the *Sluzhba* are looking for?" Surprisingly, his voice was strangely free of fear.

"I'm Father Christmas, you dumb pig farmer," Camellion growled. "What's your name and rank? I won't ask you a third time!"

He tightened his arm around the Russian's throat and pushed against the back of Prisk's head with the heel of his left hand.

"I—my name is Valentin Illich Prisk. I'm a seaman, first class, in the navy of the Union of Soviet Socialist Republics."

"I think you're a liar!" The Death Merchant jammed his arms around the man's neck. "And I don't like pig people who lie to me!"

"I'm telling you the truth!" Prisk choked out. "I can s-show you my identification. I can prove who I am and what my rank is."

"What are your duties aboard this vessel?"

Prisk hesitated for a moment, as if thinking things over. Then he said, "I'm part of the crew who's assigned to cargo watch. It's our job to make sure the cargo doesn't shift while the ship is at sea."

"Where do the ordinary crew members, such as yourself, bunk? What deck—and don't lie to me."

"Amidships, the second deck," answered Prisk in a firm voice. "But why do you want to know where the crew's quarters are? I don't understand!"

"You're not supposed to," growled the Death Merchant. "Now tell me, this ship is going to Wiese Island, isn't it? Or is there an entrance on the surface of the ocean to Zemlya II? If there is, is this ship going directly to that entrance?"

Camellion knew he had struck a vital spot in Prisk's sense of security when he felt the Russian tense.

"You're the *Amerikanski* the *Sluzhba* are looking for," Prisk said, and for the first time his voice quivered with fear. "But if I tell you anything about Zemlya II, the *Sluzhba* will shoot me as a traitor." The man's low voice shook with emotion. "Even so, I won't betray my country to an agent of capitalist imperialism!"

"I'll kill you right now if you don't tell me," warned the Death Merchant, thinking of Prisk's constant reference to the *Sluzhba*, the Russian word for "service." Practically all Russians used "service" when referring to

6

the chief border guards directorate of the KGB. "Damn you, answer me, pig farmer!"

No moron, Prisk had been putting two and two together and had come up with the correct answer, that this *Amerikanski* would have to kill him. The spy had no choice. He had already assassinated Maxim and Yuri —*he can't afford to let me live!*

Prisk did the only thing he could do; he tried to deliver the only kind of blow possible for him, considering his pretzel-like position. With all his might, he tried to jam his elbows into Camellion's stomach. He signed his own death warrant.

Becoming a vise, the Death Merchant's arm tightened tremendously around Prisk's throat, and he jerked back on the terrified Russian. At the same time he slammed the heel of his left hand against the back of the sailor's head. A snapping sound. Prisk went limp. The Big Sleep was now his forever.

The Death Merchant was extremely miserable. This was one sweet mess! Now he had three dead men on his hands. He could physically impersonate Prisk, but the other two pig farmers would be missed within a matter of hours. Then what? The big man, the one whose neck Camellion had broken with a spinning snap-twist, had red and purple shoulderboards on his coat. He was an officer. No doubt the officer in charge of the cargo checkers. The other man, whom Camellion had kicked into eternity with a *nukite* spear blow, also had to be a member of the cargo checkers.

Dragging the corpse of Prisk behind a large crate, Richard wondered whether or not the officers above decks knew that the three had gone into the hold together. In either case, Camellion knew that he would be one of the first men questioned when Maxim Geraskin and Yuri Drozdov turned up missing. No matter what action-route he took, he was damned if he did and goddamned if he didn't. Yet this game of life and death, success and failure, was like poker. You kept a straight face, hoped for the best, and played out the hand to the bitter end.

Breathing from the effort of exertion, Camellion returned to the center of the cargo hold and dragged Yuri

Drozdov behind a crate. After doing the same with Maxim Geraskin, he stripped Valentin Prisk of his uniform, removed his own clothes, and hurriedly slipped into the dead Russian's padded cottons and woolens, all the while hoping that more Ivans wouldn't come into the hold. If they did, he'd have no choice but to blow them up with the Browning and the Makarov which he had scooped up from the floor.

Working against time, the Death Merchant took a flat leather kit from a special pocket in his discarded parka. About the size of a man's travel kit, the makeup kit was all Richard needed to transform his own features into the face of Valentin Prisk. In a small way, Camellion considered himself lucky. The Russian's clothes fitted him as well as his own, and Prisk had the same kind of haircut, a kind of flat-top. Except the color was wrong. The pig farmer's hair was black; Camellion's was dark brown.

With plastic putty, adhesive pastes, and emulsion foundation, using instant-drying hair dye, compressed powders, solvents, and other liquids, Richard completed the job in less than fifteen minutes. When he was finished, the features of Richard Camellion had been miraculously transformed into the face of Valentin Prisk, even to the tiny mole above the right eyebrow.

Now somebody tell me what I'm supposed to do with my own clothes and three bodies? There was only one answer—the bilges in the ship's inner bottom. But did he have the time? *I won't know until I try, will I?*

In each cargo hold was a round man-hatch, located aft and to port, that led down to the dark, rodent-infested bilges, the hatch of number four hold being only fifty feet from where Camellion had lugged the three Russians.

Feeling like saying a prayer to the god of time, Camellion heaved the Russians, one by one, to the hatch, piling his own clothes on top of the big Ivan. He searched the corpse of Prisk and removed a billfold from the man's back pocket. Flipping it open, he looked at the identification card that had been issued by the KGB. The Russian had told the truth—his name was Valentin Prisk.

8

Richard spun the lock-wheel and threw open the hatch. The dark, round opening emitted a rancid odor and the frightened squealing of bilge rats. He first dropped his clothes into the bilge. There were three more loud splashes as the corpses of the three Russians hit the filthy water six feet below.

Camellion resealed the bilge hatch cover, then checked to make sure that the Browning Hi Power and the Makarov pistols each had a shell in the firing chamber and were switched on *safety*. Then he ran to where the clip board lay on the floor, picked it up, and began walking toward the aft bulkhead, thinking of the series of events that had led to his being in this remote area of the Soviet Union.

Saddlesoap: Two Bars, the code name for the operation, had actually begun eleven weeks ago at the Argonne National Laboratory in Chicago, Illinois. It was at A.N.L. that Camellion had met with three representatives of the National Security Agency, the deputy director of operations of the Central Intelligence Agency, the director of the CIA's Soviet bloc division, and a representative of the President of the United States.

Would Camellion undertake an extremely important mission for his government? Would he be willing to go into the Soviet Union and smuggle out a scientist who was working for the CIA? This scientist had information of such importance that, eventually, it could mean the difference between life and death for the entire United States!

Pragmatist that he was, Camellion had bluntly asked the deputy director, "Why pick me for the operation? You have more 'black cover' agents in the Soviet bloc division than in any other branch of the clandestine services."

"But none of them have your experience and know-how," the deputy director had replied.

"Nor your philosophy of life," the director of the Soviet bloc had cut in dryly. "Or rather, your philosophy of death. Staying alive is of prime importance to most of my agents."

Camellion hadn't pulled any verbal punches. "You're saying this would be practically a suicide mission."

"A regular agent would have only a ten percent margin for success in his favor," the director of the Soviet bloc had agreed. "With you, Mr. Camellion, I'd say your chances would be fifty-fifty."

"We won't argue about money," Ralph Waldo Malerle, the President's representative, had said. "If you succeed in bringing Dr. Dubanova out of the Soviet Union, we will pay you five hundred thousand dollars—all of it tax free, as you very well know. But before you decide, let me explain why it is imperative that Doctor Dubanova be brought out of the Soviet Union to this country."

Malerle went on to say that while the US was making great progress in outer space, we were far behind the USSR in learning the secrets of the world's oceans, some of which contained mountains almost as high as Mount Everest. Strangely enough (explained Malerle), while we are constantly learning about the incredible conditions surrounding our planet, about space itself, we know almost next to nothing about ocean currents and their precise movements in relationship to weather.

The vast and mysterious oceans cover three-fourths of our earth, with each nation controlling some land, but as far back as 1963, Professor G. V. Petrovich, a USSR scientist, pointed out to his colleagues, "The nation that first learns to understand the oceans will control them, and the nation that controls the seas will rule the world."

Perhaps President John F. Kennedy was thinking along the same lines when he said, some months before he was murdered, "Knowledge of the oceans is more than a matter of curiosity. Our very survival in the future may depend on it."

The world's oceans could hold the answer around which any future open conflict between the USSR and the US might revolve. Open conflict! World War III! A short but titanic struggle of unimaginable fury and horror—tremendous destruction in which scores of millions of innocent people would be vaporized into drifting atoms! Earth would be turned into a giant radioactive desert where no life could exist. Cities would stand

10

empty, like gaunt tombstones, lonely mausoleums to the memory of a two-legged idiot called man.

But on the other hand, there are scientists in the United States and in the Soviet Union who feel that final East-West struggle might take still another direction, one that is never mentioned to the public of either nation, yet one that makes your spine crawl in sheer horror.

The struggle these visionaries see would be a very quiet one, a struggle that might last for years without a single shot being fired. The deadly mushroom clouds would not rise until the very end, or perhaps not at all.

It would be a very unconventional war.

It would not be fought. It would be conducted.

It would be a war of the oceans!

The principle weapons would not be man-made, merely man-harnessed . . . the forces of nature . . . the trillions of tons of water that cover this planet.

It might be a war of weather. A knowledge of the oceans would be of vital importance in weather-control. For the earth as a whole, the ocean is the master regulator, the great stabilizer of temperature. In fact, the ocean is a savings bank for solar energy, receiving deposits in seasons of excessive insolation and paying them back in season of want.

"Are you beginning to understand, Mr. Camellion?" the deputy director had asked. The Death Merchant nodded. For years he had been interested in oceanography and knew more about the subject than the average nonscientist. He knew that without the ocean's currents our world would be visited by unthinkably harsh temperature; for the water that covers almost three-fourths of the earth's surface with an enveloping mantle is a substance of remarkable qualities. It is a wonderful absorber and radiator of heat. Because of its enormous heat capacity the ocean can absorb a great deal of heat from the sun without becoming hot, or it can lose much of its heat without becoming cold.

In short, it's the ocean's currents that distribute heat and cold over thousands of miles. It is possible to follow the course of a mass of water that originates in the trade-wind belt of the southern hemisphere and remains recognizable for a year and a half, through a course of more than 7,000 miles. Ocean currents carry hot equatorial water toward the poles and return cold water equator-ward by such surface drifts as the Labrador and the Oysahio, and even more importantly by deep currents, about which we know almost next to nothing. All this means that the oceans control the various climates of the world.

It was easy for the Death Merchant to understand that the nation that first measures and maps all the oceans' currents and comes to a precise understanding of their various effects on world weather will be in a supreme position to annihilate any enemy. By interfering with the oceans' currents by using methods yet unknown, the controlling nation could destroy an enemies' farmland, with either blistering heat, drought, or Arctic cold!

The ocean war could be one of starvation. One did not have to be a scientist to realize what would happen if our Middle West, the "bread-basket" of the nation, were turned into a desert—or hit with everlasting cold. And too little rainfall and too little food is the death-formula for any nation.

Mr. Malerle explained in a low, serious voice, "Climatologists and meteorologists know that there are parts of the world that owe their desert dryness to the very nearness of the sea, as paradoxical as this might seem. For example, the aridity of the Atacame and Kalahari deserts is curiously related to the sea, and whenever such marine deserts occur, there is always found this combination of circumstances: a western coast in the path of the prevailing winds, and a cold coastwise current. So on the west coast of South America the cold Humboldt flows, streaming northward off the shores of Chile and Peru; the offshore breezes that push these streams toward the hot lands are formed of cool air that has lain over a cool sea. As these breezes reach the land, they are forced to rise into the high coastal mountains, the ascent cooling them more than the land can warm them. As a result, there is very little condensation of water vapor, and although the cloud banks and the fogs forever promise rain, the promise is never fulfilled. The result is very clear: desert regions in certain sections of the earth.

But as Mr. Malerle quietly explained, there was far more to the silent battle for the oceans than a race for weather-control—far more. There is "deep depth mining" to be considered. Not one man in a million knows it, but vast areas of the ocean floor are strewn with crumbly lumps of very high-grade ore, some of them containing as much as fifty percent pure metal, such as iron, nickel, copper, manganese, and magnesium. In fact, more magnesium is found in just one cubic mile of seawater than man has been able to produce to date with all his ingenuity. These nodules and other minerals litter the ocean floor at an estimated $1,500,000 per square mile!

"More important to expanding populations," the director of the Russian bloc had said, "is the idea that eventually vegetable foods will come from the world's oceans. All sea plants are very nutritious and chock full of vitamins and minerals. Production would be unbelievable! For instance, on land a farmer can cultivate only on one level. In the sea, he could cultivate on all levels. A wheat farmer in Kansas might get a little more than a ton of salable grain a year per acre, but he could raise twenty-five to thirty tons of algae to an 'acre' of sea. Why, a sea farm the size of Rhode Island could feed the entire world!"

At one point during the meeting Camellion had asked, "How far are the Russians ahead of us in deep-sea research?"

None of the men could tell him! Even the CIA didn't know.

"We don't think the gap between us and the Russians is very great," the deputy director had said. "The Russkies have more than a hundred ships roaming the oceans on full-time research assignments. On the other hand, we've no more than sixty vessels, and all of our ships combined have room for only 125 to 175 scientists. A single Russian ship, the *Mikhail Lomonosov,* carries about half that many by itself. But the Soviets don't have our sophisticated deep-sea exploring devices. We have *Deepstar 4000, Aluminaut, Star I, Star II,* and other

13

highly technical craft. The Russians don't have anything to match them."

"Yet I think the Russian pig farmers are definitely ahead of us in the fish-research field," the Death Merchant had commented. "It seems I read somewhere that pig farmer fishermen off Newfoundland are now taking almost twelve times more fish that their New England rivals who have worked that area for scores of years."

The men had nodded in agreement. The director of the Soviet bloc added, "And those Russians fishing fleets do more than fish. They also map the ocean floor, check currents, and study other features of the sea, as well as make contact with Russian submarines. I'll tell you why they are ahead of us in fishing research and perhaps in current-flow studies. They are ahead because the Kremlin has its scientists working as a single highly organized unit. We don't. We don't pool our resources. We have groups and individuals all working independently of each other."

The six US Government officials had more alarming news for the Death Merchant: the Soviet submarine fleet was huge and growing—130 nuclear and 191 conventionally powered craft. Included in the 130 nuclear powered boats were a dozen giant 9,000-ton Delta class deals, each capable of launching twelve nuclear missiles 4,200 miles from the safety of the Barents Sea against any part of the United States and a large area of China. Another nineteen nuclear and seventy-seven conventionally powered subs were under construction and would see their first sea tests by the end of 1976 or the middle of 1977.

Ralph Waldo Malerle removed his glasses, and as he wiped them he mentioned that the United States Navy was looking into the future and planning to build laboratories and even entire research cities on the oceans' floors. Crews living in these underwater cities would be self-sustaining, would manufacture their own air, catch and farm their own food, and be completely independent in every manner from their surface brothers.

Malerle's voice became very serious, even sad. "But the Soviets have beaten us to it. You know of the Navy's work with Sealab I and Sealab II." He looked directly

14

into Camellion's eyes. "What the Russians have accomplished make Sealab I and Sealab II look like toys. The Soviets have built an enormous undersea city they call Zemlya II. It's located well within the Arctic Circle, in the Barents Sea, five miles west of Wiese Island; according to Dr. Dubanova, it's a marvel of scientific achievement. So you see, Mr. Camellion, those 'pig farmers,' as you call them, know more than how to slop the hogs."

The tiny wheels of logic and deduction spun rapidly within the hidden chambers of Camellion's hair-trigger mind. They were asking him to undertake what even he considered impossible.

"I suppose that next you're going to tell me that Dr. Dubanova is stationed at Zemlya II, and that I'm supposed to go there to get him?"

All six men nodded solemnly, as if they were about to pronounce a sentence of death.

"Only it's not a 'him,'" Lowell Grinnell, a NSA man, said. "It's a *her*—Dr. Raya Dubanova. She's a climatologist and an environmentalist."

Michael M. Rugg, the senior NSA man present, chimed in: "What concerns us to the extreme is that Dr. Dubanova sent word that she has a secret so important it effects the entire planet. We don't know what it is, and she's made it clear that she won't divulge it until she's safe in the United States. The real puzzler is that it isn't anything the Ivans have done. It's something they've discovered in their research involving the Poles!"

The Death Merchant merely stared at the men. How was he supposed to get to Zemlya II—swim? No, the men had explained, a nuclear submarine would carry him through the North Atlantic, on through the Denmark Straits, and finally to the Barents Sea. The sub, which would be equipped with a Gf mechanism, a newly invented device to foil Soviet detection instruments, would proceed to a point 125 miles north of Severnaya Zemlya, a group of three islands—Komsomolets Island, to the north; October Revolution Island, which was the middle island; and Bolshevik Island, the last island to the south.

From the 125 mile point, Camellion and two Russian-speaking CIA agents would proceed by a tiny submarine, of the Perry Submarine type, to Bolshevik Island. Why this roundabout route? Because Stryelka, the only good-sized town on Bolshevik Island, served as the main supply base for Zemlya II, which was 384 miles to the north-west!

How would the Death Merchant and his two men get to Zemlya II from Stryelka? That would be Camellion's problem. Uncle Sam was paying him half a million bucks to figure out that minor detail! How he and the two CIA boys would escape with Dr. Dubanova was also his problem! Oh yes, one more thing. NSA also wanted him to learn the exact location of the twelve Delta class nuclear subs stationed somewhere in the Barents Sea!

"You're all nuts!" Camellion had flatly told the officials.

I'm even nuttier! he thought, walking up the stairway to the open deck of the *Mikhail Lomonosov*.
Because—here I am!

Chapter Two

On his way to the main deck, the Death Merchant met half a dozen other comrades, but they ignored him and continued on their various ways. At least the sheer size of the *Mikhail Lomonosov* was in his favor. The huge, odd-looking vessel, which had three superstructures —bow, midships, and stern—carried a crew of 1100 men. Plus how many scientists and technicians????

No! Camellion reminded himself. Such reasoning was false security. No matter how many Russians were aboard the *Mikhail Lomonosov*, there were still those who knew Valentin Prisk. There were the man's superiors to contend with—*And I don't even know their names or what they look like?* In a way, Camellion felt like a man who had just been told by his doctor that he needed a prostatectomy and that the operation might

16

result in retrograde ejaculation. *I'm in the same fix! I don't know whether I'm coming or going!*

Camellion wasn't worried about his Prisk "falseface"; he had supreme confidence in his ability as a makeup artist. He was the Rembrandt of plastic putty—and knew it. His new face would have fooled Prisk's own mother.

With the bitter wind slashing at his face around the hood of his parka, he headed toward the midships superstructure, the darkness of the polar afternoon broken only by the lights stretched out along the deck. At this northern end of the world the wind vied with the long night in making life difficult; however, the Soviets had learned to cope with the hostile conditions. The 54,000 people of Stryelka, on Bolshevik Island, were experts at it. The toddlers had sunlamps in their schools, for example. They'd strip down to their undies, don dark goggles, and parade around in the eerie violet iridescence while baking front and backsides. All schoolchildren and all office and factory workers received the same treatment during the 2½ month polar night—one week in mid-November to wean them from the sun that had just gone, and one week in late January to prepare for its return.

While Camellion had wandered around Stryelka, he had noticed the special construction techniques employed to break the force of the constant wind. Each new apartment complex was enclosed on three sides, and kindergartens and schools were built inside the almost windless "microclimate" created by the tall, zigzagging wings. Complexes were formed into self-sufficient "microdistricts," with shops and other services all within short walks. Electricity was used for cooking because the burning of gas depleted oxygen from the buildings, since windows were always sealed.

Always there was the bitter cold, the raw, restless wind, and the darkness. Even during the long polar day in summer, the sun would never climb higher than forty-two degrees in the sky. The growing season was so short —snow fell ten months of the year—that eighty percent of dairy fodder was shipped in to the three islands of Severnaya Zemlya. A constellation of hothouses supplemented fresh vegetable imports.

17

Man's body joined his brain in coping with the harshness of the climate. His blood became thicker because of the sustained cold. After a year of such cold, the hemoglobin content would rise to seventy percent to ninety-six percent above normal to improve oxygen transport; yet basic body rhythms, such as menstrual cycles, remained unaffected.

The Death Merchant's question of where to go, and how to act after he got there, was unexpectedly answered as he turned into a gangway leading to the boat deck of the midship superstructure. Coming toward him, a tall, sharp-faced man, dressed in heavy parka, boots and gloves, glared angrily at Richard.

"Valentin, where have you been?" the man whispered harshly, blocking Camellion's path. "You're almost forty-five minutes late. Damn it, you know what a fanatic Comrade Nardrokin is about schedules and security! Now we have to explain to him why you're late! What's the matter with you, Valentin?" The man leaned closer and lowered his voice. "You don't have a bottle hidden down in the holds, do you? And where are Maxim and Yuri? Comrade Nardrokin is about ready to start searching for them!"

Camellion did some hair-trigger analyzing. Whoever the man was, he hadn't addressed Camellion as "comrade." Nor had the man used a last name; therefore, he wasn't an officer. Officers in the Red Army always used an underling's full name. *And the fact that he called me "Valentin," Prisk's first name, and is talking to me on a personal basis, indicates he's a personal friend. But who is Comrade Nardokin? The officer in charge of the cargo checkers?*

"I had trouble with the inventory." Camellion did his best to imitate the voice of Prisk. "I had to triple-check the figures."

The other man peered closely at Camellion, at the man he assumed was Valentin Prisk. "After we see Comrade Nardrokin, you had better check in at the dispensary. Your voice sounds odd; you might be coming down with a viral infection. But where are Yuri and Maxim? Are they still down there or what?"

Camellion said the only thing he could. "They're

18

still down below. At least they were when I left. That's all I know."

The Russian regarded Camellion with a puzzled expression.

"I don't understand any of this," he said. "We all know how Comrade Nardrokin is. That's why the bosses in Moscow gave him this assignment: because he's such a son of a bitch." The man shook his head. "The three of you will have some explaining to do to him. We might as well go to his office and get it over with."

The Russian turned, and Camellion, thinking of what the man had said about the bosses in Moscow, followed him along the gangway, through a door that opened into the superstructure, and finally into a ward room where men were lounging around, drinking tea and hot chocolate. Some were playing chess, others reading or amusing themselves in other ways. None of them paid any attention to Camellion and the comrade with him as they removed their gloves and parkas.

After hanging up his parka, the Russian with Camellion turned and looked at Camellion, then drew back slightly as if seeing a ghost. Richard noted the surprised expression on the man's face—*does he know?*

Poised for instant action, Richard in turn faked surprise.

"Anything the matter?" he brazenly asked.

"No, nothing," the Russian said quickly. (*Too quickly!* thought the Death Merchant.) "I only wanted to remind you not to forget your clipboard. Comrade Nardrokin will demand to see the check-list." With a nod of his head he indicated the board that Camellion had laid on a table. "Come, let's go report to Comrade Nardrokin."

The Death Merchant nodded, picked up the clipboard, and followed the man across the room and out the door into a long hallway. He knew the Russian had lied and that something was wrong. But what? *My face is perfect; I'm the perfect image of Prisk. So what is it?*

Camellion had noticed that his Russian wore a dark blue seaman's uniform that had one more stripe on its sleeve than the uniform Richard wore, the one he had taken from Valentin Prisk, indicating that the comrade was a grade higher than Prisk and Drozdov and Geraskin.

He's probably responsible for their actions, which explains his concern about my being late and his being worried about what Comrade Nardrokin might do.

The Russian hurried down the long passageway, the Death Merchant following, clipboard in hand. Camellion knew instinctively where they were going when they turned a corner and he saw two guards sitting on chairs in front of a door, Dragunov submachine guns across their laps, Stechkin machine pistols in polished hip holsters. On their other hip was another holster, this one filled with an odd-looking weapon that resembled an oversized flashlight. The Death Merchant's eyes narrowed when he saw the stun guns, or Tasers. *Well, well . . . the pig farmers are getting sophisticated!* Camellion thought, as he speculated on the weapon which had been invented in the United States by Jack Cover. The Taser, powered by six rechargeable nickel-cadmium batteries, fired two barbs attached to eighteen feet of fine wires. Should the barbs hit a person, a three-watt, 50,000-volt charge would leap through the closed circuit, the severe shock instantly disrupting the victim's nervous system, smashing him into unconsciousness. Muscular control returned after the Taser was switched off, and there were no after-effects.

The two guards wore bright blue uniforms. They were KGB, the insignia on their collars telling Camellion they were attached to the Political Security Service of the KGB. Now the Death Merchant knew who Comrade Nardrokin was. He was the KGB political officer on board the *Mikhail Lomonosov*—the last man in the world the Death Merchant wanted to see!

The Russian with Camellion presented his identification to the two guards, and Camellion did likewise. One of the guards nodded, and Camellion's companion knocked on the door, which was opened by one of the two guards inside the office. Once inside, Camellion saw that neither guard carried submachine guns. They were armed only with pistols and Tasers.

Felix B. K. Nardrokin sat behind a steel desk

cluttered with papers. On one corner of the desk was a vase of paper flowers. Broad-shouldered, stocky, he had a jowly, seamed face and an abrasive personality to match his pugnacious appearance. Unlike the guards, he was neatly dressed in a baggy brown suit.

Seeing Camellion and his Russian companion, Nardrokin smiled evilly, leaned back in his chair, and folded his arms across his chest.

"So, Comrade Josef Gemki," he said to the man with Camellion, "I see that you have found him." He glared at Camellion. "Very well, Comrade Prisk. What is your explanation? Why did it take—"

"Comrade Nardrokin, he's not Comrade Prisk!" Josef Gemki cut in fiercely. He moved back from Camellion and pointed a finger at him. "I don't know who he is, but he's an impostor! He's not Valentin Prisk! He has to be an imperialist spy!"

Felix Nardrokin leaned forward, his shaggy brows forming a deep V of astonishment, his eyes opening wide in alarm and disbelief. The two guards behind Camellion instantly became alert and jerked their attention to the Death Merchant, who faked total amazement as he turned to Josef Gemki.

"Comrade, are you out of your mind? What do you mean, I'm not Valentin Prisk? Who else can I be?"

"Yes! Explain yourself Comrade Gemki!" demanded Nardrokin, getting to his feet. "You are acting uncivilized. I can see for myself that this man is Comrade Prisk!"

"I am not acting uncivilized, Comrade Nardrokin!" Gemki said angrily, staring furiously at Camellion. "This man looks like Comrade Prisk, but I know that he is not. Look at the little finger on his right hand. This man has a full finger. Comrade Prisk had only half of his little finger. A few years ago Comrade Prisk got his finger caught in a machine, and half of the finger was amputated. Your file on Comrade Prisk will prove I am right!"

Ah, so that's what the pig farmer noticed when I removed my gloves! Camellion thought, cursing himself. He had been so intent on noting the details of Prisk's face that he hadn't noticed the man's fingers. *Well, hell!*

21

Nobody has ever been perfect, except Jesus Christ. And look how he ended up!

Knowing that the fat was in the Soviet fire, the Death Merchant swung into action. Nardrokin screamed "Arrest him." as the guards were pulling pistols from their holsters, Camellion spun and chopped the nearest guard across the bridge of the nose with the long edge of the clipboard, the slicing blow smashing the frontal bone of the hog farmer's skull and switching off his consciousness. A moment later Richard grabbed the right wrist of the second guard, who had managed to draw his Stechkin machine pistol, and kneed him with such force in the groin that the pain made the man's eyes almost pop out of his head. The machine pistol slipped from his right hand and fell to the floor. The guard, his guts exploding with agony, was utterly helpless against the speed and power of the Death Merchant. Using the man's arm as a lever, Richard flung him into a stunned Josef Gemki. Both Gemki and the guard fell heavily against the front of the desk, their bodies blocking the view of Felix Nardrokin. The fierce-faced political officer had jerked a Tokarev automatic pistol from a drawer and was trying to aim it at the man posing as Valentin Prisk. But by the time Nardrokin jerked to the right to fire around Gemki and the guard, he was too late.

Richard Camellion dropped to the floor, scooped up the Stechkin m.p. dropped by the guard, twisted around in the direction of Comrade Nardrokin, raised the weapon, and pulled the trigger. The 9mm bullet banged into Nardrokin's skull and broke his brain. An instant dead man, he sagged to the floor. Josef Gemki and the guard followed him on the other side of the desk.

Twice more the machine pistol in Camellion's hand roared. The first slug tore into the guard's belly, cut apart his colon, and shattered his right hip. The second 9mm slug hit Josef Gemki in his left side, tore through his lungs and heart, made its exit out his right side, and buried itself in a picture of Lenin hanging on the wall, putting a nice round hole in the chin of the father of the Russian Revolution.

Hearing the three loud shots, the two KGB guards in

the corridor charged into the office, the door flying open before the lifeless bodies had time to hit the floor. Having expected the two nitwits, the Death Merchant switched the machine pistol to full automatic and pulled the trigger, the Stechkin belching out the remainder of its clip. Four slugs knifed into the first guard, putting him to sleep forever. The last two 9mms hit the second guard in the side and in the chest, ending his life as he tried to swing his submachine gun around to Camellion. Then it was all over. Blood pouring from their mouths, the two KGB guards sagged to the floor.

Hot double damn! I can't kill the entire ship, but I can take a lot of them with me before I go bye bye into deathland!

Richard pulled the two machine pistols from the holsters of the guards he had just killed, jammed them underneath his tunic into his belt, then took five Stechkin clips from the ammo pouch of each guard and placed them in the breast pockets of his jacket.

His mind swung into overdrive. Cold-bloodedly he admitted that he was as good as dead. The thought didn't really bother him, since he considered death as normal as birth. You come in one way and go out the other. It's only a question of when and how—and how you go is far more important than when!

Camellion did some hard thinking. The superstructure toward the bow of the vessel was devoted to oceanography; it belonged to the scientists aboard the *Mikhail Lomonosov*. The actual operation of the ship was conducted from the superstructure located toward the stern. Here were the bridge and chart room, the engineering offices and the radio room. Richard was determined to gain entrance to the radio room and flash out a short message to *Albacore*, the United States nuclear sub submerged 125 miles north of Severnaya Zemlya. No matter what high frequency band the *Mikhail Lomonosov* used, the sophisticated radio equipment of the sub would pick up the message—but only if *Albacore* had the tip of its antenna above water. Camellion supposed that in the long run, it didn't really matter—*The mission is a bust and I'm a dead man.* Surrender? Not a chance!

Camellion picked up one of the Dragunov submachine guns dropped by the guards, stepped out into the hall, and saw that more pig farmers were converging on the office from both directions. At sight of him both groups jerked up short in confusion, not knowing whether Camellion was on their side or the enemy.

Richard didn't wait for the Russians to make up their minds. Holding the Dragunov at hip level, he sprayed the first group with a long, snarling burst, then dropped and rolled over to the wall in time to avoid a swarm of slugs from the other group in the hall. Then he swung the tommy gun around and opened fire, the stream of 7.62mm steel ripping the Russians into shreds of red blood and blue uniforms, the echo of the exploding cartridges ringing up and down the hall, which was already hazy with fumes and the sharp odor of burnt gunpowder.

Wu-weeeee! Wu-weeeee! The danger alarm began ringing all over the vessel. Richard got to his feet and raced in the direction of the stern, jumping through a half-dozen fresh corpses as he headed down the hall. He charged around a corner and ran down a stairway that would take him to the first deck that was actually inside the vessel. His chances of reaching the radio room were almost nonexistent, but on the main deck, right out in the open, he wouldn't have any chance. The pig farmers could cut him to pieces from the superstructure. At the same time he wanted to avoid the crew's quarters, not only because he wanted to avoid needless killing, but because he wanted to conserve ammo. No doubt the crew's quarters were on the third or fourth deck level.

Reaching the second deck, Camellion saw that he was in another long corridor. Six to eight feet ahead was a double stairway—one flight leading upward, the other, downward.

Fudge! Coming toward him, from each end of the hallway, were more Russkies, armed to the teeth with pistols, submachine guns, and Tasers.

The Death Merchant made a dive for the stairs that slanted downward just as the group of Russians to the left fired. Right then and there Camellion would have been a dead man had it not been for his Kevlar-Thermacoactyl underwear—his long johns, which were lighter than nylon but warmer than wool—and tougher than steel. Composed of seven layers, the underwear was bulletproof and could stop even a .44 Auto-Mag slug at point blank range, the knit layers absorbing the shock, although the material would leave its imprint on the slug as it flattened out and fell harmlessly away.

From his wrists to his ankles, Camellion was bullet-proof—and a good thing, too. Just as his body was about to hit the opening of the stairway, five slugs stabbed into his clothing. A 9mm Stechkin hit his right outer thigh! Another 9mm punched him in the right rib cage! A 7.62mm Dragunov bullet blasted him in the right shoulder, while two more 7.62mms plowed into the inside calf of his left leg—the force of the five making Camellion feel as though he had been struck by a bull-dozer and slamming him against the railing on the opposit side of the stairs.

"We got him! He's hit!" Camellion heard a Russian yell in triumph. Quickly recovering, his entire right side aching, Richard half-crawled and half-fell to the bottom of the stairs, thinking that he was a kind of flesh and blood tire. *Ironic! Just like Kevlar!* That's why Du Pont had developed Kevlar—as a substitute for steel in belted radial tires.

Richard looked up and down the hallway of the second deck. The corridor was empty. He moved to the side of the stairway, looked upward, waited, and fired when the first Ivans appeared at the top of the stairs. The torrent of hot steel ripped through four Russians as easily as high velocity slugs could tear through toilet paper.

Two Russian roosters screamed as bullets bored into their lower bellies. Another silly Slavic simply folded at the knees and flopped to the floor, his peaked officer's cap in shreds, the top of his head shattered and oozing blood, chipped bone, and gray white brain matter. He pitched down the stairs headfirst, his Dra-gunov chatterbox clanking down the steps after him.

"He's not dead!" one of the Russians yelled.

No, hog caller, I'm not! To keep the other Stalin stupids from rushing the mouth of the stairs, Richard sprayed the sides of the entrance, exhausting all the ammo in the Dragunov's banana-shaped clip. He tossed aside the useless weapon, ran to the front of the stairs, and picked up the chatterbox dropped by the Russian who had slid down the steps.

A hell of a way to spend a December afternoon! Camellion turned to stern, and there they were, down the hallway—more Russians, who dropped to the deck and opened fire. The Death Merchant jumped out of range to the right, in front of the steps, firing upward again at the determined Ivans attempting to storm the mouth of the stairs.

It was like a Mexican standoff gone sour! Just as Camellion cut loose with a long burst of 7.62mm slugs, one of the Russians aimed straight down at Richard and pulled the trigger of a machine pistol that was on full automatic. The Death Merchant's blast opened up the Russian and cut apart four of his comrades. The Commie creep with the Stechkin cried out, died, and pitched down the bloody steps, along with two of his companions, who were as lifeless as he was. The other two Ivans sank into hell at the top of the steps, weapons sliding from their stiffening fingers.

As for Mrs. Camellion's son Richard, the ten 9mm Stechkin slugs, tearing pieces of cloth from his jacket as they bored into the material, had struck him full in the chest, each slug not more than a quarter of an inch away from its predecessor. The combined force of the slugs pitched Camellion six feet back and forced him to cry out from the terrific blow, even though he was not actually injured. The slugs mushroomed out, flattening themselves out against the steel-like fabric of the Kevlar-Thermacoactyl underwear.

In spite of the blow—it felt like an atomic bomb—Camellion did not lose track of his amazing sense of self-preservation, that well-honed instinct which had saved his life hundreds of times all over the world. Down on one knee, he sent a short blast at the mouth of the stairs, then jerked his body to the left, From around the lower part of the steps he triggered off a stream of Dragunov steel at the Russkies trying to rush him from down the hallway. The swarm of 7.62 slugs buzzed out

26

three of the Ivans instantly, the slugs tearing through one man and mortally wounding a fourth, who dropped his submachine gun, fell against the wall, and sagged like an empty sack to the deck. The remaining two sailors proved they were rank amateurs in a fire-fight. They should have kept firing as they dropped. They didn't. They stopped firing, dropped to the deck—and died! During that split second lag-time Camellion had blown away their lives.

Richard jumped to his feet. He was about to run sternways down the corridor when he spotted a blue-clad Russian staring out from around a corner of the hall. The man ducked back before Camellion could ice him out. Not that it made too much difference. The crud probably had half a dozen helpers with him. Either way, the passage to the stern was blocked— *And my music box is empty! Either I go to another deck level to find a route to the superstructure at the stern, or else I have to retreat toward the bow of this tub—hell!*

Camellion tossed aside the useless Dragunov, pulled the two Stechkin machine pistols from underneath his tattered jacket, turned, and looked down the other end of the hall. Twenty feet to his right was another hall, this one intersecting and horizontal to the one in which he stood. Camellion turned and looked behind him. No Russians. This group of Commies was playing it cool. He ran to the corner of the intersecting hallway and looked around it—empty. The corridor stretched out for twenty feet before making an abrupt turn toward the bow.

The Death Merchant pondered for a moment. He didn't know where he was going, but under the prevailing circumstances, with the Russians right behind him, did it matter?

He moved quickly down the length of the horizontal corridor and was about to flatten himself against a wall to peer around its corner when a dozen Russians charged from around the corridor pointed toward the bow—so close to the Death Merchant that they almost collided with him, and he with them!

The Russians were fast. Camellion was faster, blowing

27

up two sailors with Stechkin slugs before they could even level their submachine guns at him. With slugs in their chests, the two dead dummies fell against their comrades, one of whom managed to press the firing bar of his Taser as he fell sideways against the wall.

The Lenin louse looked stunned, then flabbergasted as the stun gun buzzed. The two barbs shot out at the ends of their thin wires and buried themselves in the Death Merchant's shattered jacket. Fifty thousand volts coursed through Camellion's clothing, the current at three watts. But Camellion's bulletproof underwear prevented the barbs from touching his skin and the voltage could not reach his body.

The Russian's mouth fell open in astonishment when Camellion brushed aside the two thin wires attached to the barbs and erased his face with a 9mm Stechkin slug.

It was then that the Death Merchant's luck went all bad. Another Russian aimed his Taser and pressed down on the firing bar. The Russian's aim was perfect. The barbs shot out, and this time they fastened themselves in Camellion's neck, just below his left ear.

There was no escape. This time 50,000 volts spread to every cell of Camellion's body. For a fraction of a second he felt as if he were being torn apart, as though his very brain were in the process of exploding, of disintegrating. Then an ocean of blackness engulfed him, the tidal wave of blackness drowning his consciousness.

Chapter Three

His hands handcuffed behind his back, Richard Camellion sat on the chair in the middle of the cell, staring at the two guards in front of him on either side of the door. Capturing him, two days ago, had been relatively easy. The Taser charge had knocked him out.

By the time he had regained consciousness, he had found himself staring into the deadly muzzles of pistols and submachine guns, while a KGB agent probed his mouth for a suicide pill.

He had been handcuffed, dragged to a cell somewhere in the bowels of the vessel, and stripped and carefully searched by agents attached to the KGB. The men expressed great interest in his bulletproof underwear and in the fact that his face was the identical image of Valentin Prisk.

Realizing that Camellion's face was a clever job of makeup, the agents dissolved the grease paint with alcohol and other solvents and removed the molded plastic putty from his cheeks, mouth, and chin. They stared at his real face in amazement after the job of removal had been completed.

Captain Paul Yubishkanonavitch, a thin-faced man with cruel gray eyes and a sharply pointed chin, had come to the call to question Camellion, demanding that he identify himself, confess for whom he was working, and why he was on board the *Makhail Lomonosov*.

Camellion merely smiled at the man who had been Felix Nardrokin's assistant. "You know I'm not going to tell you one damn thing," he had replied. He had fully expected to be tortured, but Yubishkanonavitch, while visibly annoyed, had only commented, "Your behavior is typical of a bourgeois. All class enemies are stubborn. But you'll answer all the questions put to you once you get to Moscow. You're a professional. I don't have to convince you that we have time-tested ways that are most effective in making a bourgeois like yourself talk."

"Hmmm, then it seems I shall get to see the new headquarters of the KGB first chief directorate," Camellion had mused. "I understand it's hidden off a circumferential highway outside Moscow?"

Captain Yubishkanonavitch ignored Camellion's droll humor.

"We already know you're the third foreign agent who came to Northern Land only a week ago, no doubt by minisubmarine," he said smugly. "We found the bodies of the other two spies. They were frozen to death. How you managed to ever reach Stryelka and get aboard this ship, how you managed to elude our patrols and survive—you will reveal all the details in due course! Of course, such a task would not be too difficult for the Death Merchant, now would it?"

"What's the Northern Land? I never heard of it."

Captain Yubishkanonavitch finished lighting a cigarette and blew smoke in Camellion's direction. "Come, come, my friend! There is no use in pretending with me. You speak perfect Russian. You're well aware that Severnaya Zemlya means 'Northern Land' in the Russian language. It is also a sheer waste of time to pretend you are not the Death Merchant!"

Inwardly cursing his rotten luck, Camellion forced a loud snicker. "So that's who you think I am—the Death Merchant! That's some joke!"

"No one but the Death Merchant could have done what you did," Yubishkanonavitch said. "And with such a small but complete makeup kit"—he pointed to the leather package that one of the KGB agents was holding —"who else but the Death Merchant has the talent to transform his face into the identical face of another, such as you did? You are the Death Merchant!"

"Have it your way," Camellion mumbled.

"We also suspect the nature of your mission: to get to Zemlya II. Yes, you will get to our underwater city, *Amerikanski*, but not in the way you and your CIA masters anticipated. From Zemlya II you will be flown to Moscow for trial. There you will be executed by a firing squad, not only because you are a spy, but for the murders you committed aboard this ship."

Yubishkanonavitch and his agents took Camellion's fingerprints, and photographed him from all angles, the procedures making Camellion furious and instilling in him a deep sense of frustration. He had never before been identified by the KGB. To worldwide Russian intelligence he had only been a name. Now the pig farmers not only had his fingerprints, but even knew what he looked like! This realization, coupled with the knowledge that escape was impossible, made him wish he could have a fatal heart attack.

At no time was he left alone in the cell. Always there

were two guards at the door, their hands on Stechkin machine pistols. Never were the handcuffs removed from his wrists, except when he had to use the toilet bucket, or when they brought him his meals, which usually consisted of boiled buckwheat porridge, and little dough-covered meatballs. Other times, he was given soup or Russian pancakes made with flour, milk, eggs, butter, and yeast.

Each time he ate or had to use the toilet two more guards would come into the cell, their Stechkins drawn. While one man would unlock his handcuffs, the other three would stand back, two with deadly machine pistols, the third with a Taser. The stun gun would have been more than enough, for all that Camellion wore was a pair of coveralls the Ivans had given him. He was even barefooted; however, the cell was amply heated.

The two extra guards also came into the cell when it came time for Camellion to sleep. Then, his wrists and ankles were handcuffed to the cot, forcing him to sleep on his back—or lie awake and curse his fate.

The Death Merchant had no choice but to conclude that he wasn't going anyplace, except where the Russians wanted him to go. All he could do was sit like a dummy (or lie as straight as a corpse) and think of how *Saddlesoap: Two Bars* had fallen into failure.

The trip in the *Albacore* across the North Atlantic had gone off without a hitch. The sleek nuclear submarine, skippered by Commander Merrill Stacher, had made its way expertly through the Denmark Straits and had reached the bleak Barents Sea. Without any difficulty, *Albacore* had proceeded to the coordinates 125 miles north of Komsomolets Island, the most northern island of the Severnaya Zemlya group.

The Gf mechanism had worked perfectly. Half a dozen times, the Asdic aboard the *Albacore* had detected the presence of Russian U-boats in the area, but such a discovery had not been followed by any unusual activity or maneuvering on the part of the Russian U-boats, which would have been the case had the pig farmers discovered the *Albacore*. Conclusion: the Gf mechanism worked—and if enemy subs couldn't detect *Albacore,* neither could Russian surface vessels.

The Gf device had been invented around the discovery, in 1964, that low frequency sound waves travel through water for a much longer time and distance than high frequency waves. From this discovery came the United States Navy's Project Artemis, a sort of underwater DEW line using sound instead of radar. Since then, the United States Navy had gotten the idea that it could "bug" the ocean with giant transducers which would constantly send out large volumes of low frequency sound, which would fan out in all directions. Then, when the sounds struck a solid object, they would bounce right back to listening posts along the United States shores. The waves of sound would then be translated by computers, and if they couldn't be identified as something harmless, attack subs and aircraft would investigate.

The sound waves would have to be translated, because the ocean is not a dark and silent place, in spite of what most people think. In the depths, it is dark, but far from silent, being actually an incredibly noisy place. There are creatures that groan, grunt, rumble, whistle, scream and squeak.

For years the United States Navy had worked to find some way of cataloging the weird sounds so that it could tell the difference between them and the subdued motors of an enemy sub—had worked and had failed.

The Gf mechanism was a by-product of this research. The "G" part of the mechanism somehow distributed the sound of the sub's motors among the other sounds of the ocean, while the "f" part used both kinds of sounds in a manner that shielded the hull of the sub from magnemometers and other detectors. The Gf mechanism was one of the United States Navy's top secrets, and practically speaking, it made the *Albacore* invisible.

Sitting there in the cell, the Death Merchant reflected on how well the mission had gone until he and Jesse Tripp and Roger Daley, the two CIA agents who were to accompany him, had begun the final lap in a Dy-7K Perry Cubmarine, their goal the lonely wind-swept western shore of October Revolution Island, the middle island of the Severnaya Zemlya group.

Disaster struck thirty-one miles from shore, when the variable ballast control system of the cubmarine began to malfunction.

"We can make it to shore," Jesse Tripp had said, "but the way the rocks and current are off October Revolution Island, we might sink before we have time to get out. Our scuba gear is good for only four hundred feet, and right off shore the depth is almost twelve hundred feet. Gentlemen, we're in one hell of a spot!"

In desperation, Camellion and the two men pored over their Marine maps of Severnaya Zemlya, finally deciding that their best chance would be to head for one of the tiny inland coves on the western coast of Bolshevik Island, the last island to the south of the three-island "Northern Land" group. In these coves the current was far less violent and there were no large rocks against which the cubmarine could be smashed; yet the new route would greatly increase the chances of their being discovered.

In scuba suits, dragging their equipment behind them, the Death Merchant and the two CIA men managed to swim to Bolshevik Island. One mishap, going ashore, and there would have been no salvation, not in waters where the temperature was a subfreezing 26.4 degrees. An hour after they left the cubmarine, the vehicle sank to the bottom of the cove, an automatically set device opening the three valves of the ballast tanks.

On shore, the temperature was forty-one degrees below zero. While they were setting up the small Urethane tent, the wind suddenly gusted to thirty-five miles per hour, giving them a wind-chill factor of almost eighty-two degrees below zero. Within the confines of the tent they changed into Russian-made parkas and all the other kinds of clothing one needs to survive when almost a thousand miles north of the Arctic Circle. Included in their equipment were AK assault rifles equipped with Desvov silencers, and cards and papers identifying them as citizens who lived in Stryelka and worked in the coal mines of Bolshevik Island.

They had buried the scuba gear and the tent and

had proceeded to move in the direction of Stryelka, nine miles to the south.

Four hours later Camellion and Tripp and Daley had been spotted by a KGB ski patrol. In the ensuing exchange of gunfire, Tripp was wounded. Camellion and the two CIA agents escaped the patrol, but Tripp was so weak Camellion and Daley were forced to abandon him. Hours later, the Death Merchant had been forced to leave Daley after the man had been wounded in a gunbattle with another KGB ski patrol. Again, the Death Merchant escaped. By ambushing a lone Russian soldier and disguising himself as the pig farmer, he reached Stryelka, one of the Soviet Union's most booming frontier cities. For over thirty years the Russians had worked the enormous coal veins surrounding the city, and off shore were numerous oil drilling platforms, some of which could drill as many as seven wells from one position. What irked Camellion was that the platforms were of the monopod variety and were as modern as anything he had seen in the United States. But as Ralph Waldo Malerle had said months before, "Those pig farmers know more than how to slop the hogs."

Several days after reaching Stryelka Camellion had smuggled himself aboard the huge *Mikhail Lomonosov*, hidden in a pallet that had contained crates of frozen cabbages. He had not chosen the vessel out of sheer accident, nor out of desperation either. Almost two weeks earlier, before *Albacore* had reached the 125-mile coordinates north of Komsomolets Island, the Office of Naval Intelligence had flashed a top secret coded message to the sub that the *Mikhail Lomonosov* was one of the vessels that often made a run to Wiese Island. Zemlya II was only five miles west of Wiese Island.

Now, what difference did it make? Tripp and Daley were dead. The Death Merchant had been captured. *Saddle Soap: Two Bars* had failed. In fact, no mission ever attempted by Richard Camellion had ever fallen apart so quickly and so completely!

Here I sit, handcuffed and wearing a pair of coveralls a size too large for me. But like the Good Book is fond of saying, "There will be balm and bitterness."

Or—"Rise and renew your strength. Harken to the voice of my cry!" Uh huh. Too bad Jesus Christ and all the wild-eyed prophets didn't have to deal with these Russian pig farmers. To hell with speculation. Here I am and there isn't anything I can do about it!

The Death Merchant was equally helpless when the *Mikhail Lomonosov* docked at Wiese Island and he was removed from the vessel and taken ashore. Because of the heavy sleeves of the parka and the thick gloves on Camellion's hands, handcuffs would not fit around his wrists. Instead, before taking him from the cell, the KGB guards looped lengths of dog chain around his wrists, ankles, and neck. That is how they led him from the *Mikhail Lomonosov*, like a wild animal, with five agents holding the ends of the chains. Nonetheless, the Death Merchant kept his eyes open, cataloging each tiny detail of everything he saw. Not that there was much to see.

Only 9.4 miles in diameter at its widest point, Wiese Island was nothing but a speck of ice and snow in the lower Arctic Ocean. Its only value to the Soviet Union was that it was in a convenient position for a meteorological and radar station. From their cold-weather base on Wiese Island, the forever suspicious Russians could monitor the entire North Pole area, just in case the *Amerikanskis* might be up to something.

As Camellion was led to a large jeep with extra large tires, he noticed that the dock was very modern. The facilities included ten piers, each one large enough to accommodate any kind of ocean-going vessel. Furthermore, there were four enormous roller-type dock cranes, indicating that a lot of tremendously heavy equipment was often unloaded.

Other than the gray painted warehouselike buildings close to the docks there was nothing to see but a couple of dozen prefabricated buildings standing a short distance away, each over a hundred feet long. Their roofs were covered with snow, and they were all widely separated as a precaution against fire. All the buildings were covered with snow except the dome housing the radar to track weather balloons. There were four short-wave radio towers and a large helicopter pad, on which rested a dozen Mi-8 helicopters, dependable crafts powered by a single 2,700 s.h.p. Soloviev turboshaft engine driving a four-blade rotor. That was all, except small two-man snowmobiles and huge trucks with tracks instead of wheels.

Technically, the base on Wiese Island was known as *Sovietskaya Station I. Sovietskaya II* was located on Ushakov Island, 121 miles to the north of Wiese. Camellion was familiar with many facts about Sovietskaya Station 1, which was 384 miles northwest of Severnaya Zemlya. In such a severe climate, Russian personnel was rotated every three months, the intense cold causing the men to suffer from headaches, shortness of breath, pounding of the heart, and low blood pressure. Because of the elevation, the boiling point inside the nonmagnetic huts (built without iron to avoid affecting magnetic observations) was so low that pressure cookers had to be used for cooking. When the mercury hit bottom, strange things would happen. Water, dropped on the supercooled ice outside, danced as though it were on a hot stove, breaking up into droplets that froze into so many tiny pearls. Kerosene looked like wet snow. Special oils had to be used in machines. When going outside during this time of the year—midwinter—every man wore a face mask that provided electronically heated air; their clothing was also heated, fifty-watt pocket-sized batteries sending current through coils distributed throughout the material of their parkas and pants. Even their boots and gloves were plugged in to the batteries that were carried in special pockets in the parkas.

Snug and comfortable in their heated suits, Camellion, the five KGB guards, and Captain Paul Yubishkanonavitch drove in the enclosed jeep to the helicopter pad, where they boarded a Mi-8 helicopter that was soon airborne and headed east, toward the opposite side of the island. Why? Why are we going in this direction? Looking out the window next to him, all Richard could see were scattered snow-heavy trees and rocky snow and ice-covered terrain.

"I rather gather that you're not flying me first class to China," Camellion quipped to Yubishkanonavitch who was sitting next to him. "Or am I not supposed to know where we're going?"

"It's no secret," Yubishkanonavitch said blandly, glancing at the the Death Merchant. "I told you days ago that you would be going to Zemlya II. We will begin the journey from the other side of the island. That's all you need to know."

"Don't be impatient, Death Merchant," laughed one of the guards, a Mongolian type named Paruir Lovaya, who was from the Uzbek section of the central Asian region of the Soviet Union. "You will be executed soon enough. They will make short work of you in Moscow."

The Mi-8 helicopter hadn't been in the air for more than six or seven minutes before it began to lose altitude as its pilot prepared to land. *It doesn't add up!* Camellion thought. But he knew that it did. *I'm just not using the right adding machine.* But why land here? Below was nothing but barren wilderness, nothing but wind-torn trees and jagged rocks perpetually covered with ice and snow. Ahead, not more than a mile, were snow-covered hills whose eastern sides overlooked the endless stretch of the Arctic Ocean.

Captain Yubishkanonavitch, seeing the puzzlement in Richard's eyes, called out lightheartedly to the pilot, "Move several hundred feet to the right. I want this bourgeois *Amerikanski* to see that when it comes to technology, we are aristocrats."

The Death Merchant felt like laughing—*So he wants me to see what an upper class race of people the Russians are, does he? That's as ridiculous as an Eskimo wanting to discuss calculus with Einstein!*

Camellion didn't feel like laughing when the pilot swung the helicopter to the right, hovered the craft, and Yubishkanonavitch turned and smiled.

"Look out your window, Death Merchant," he said smugly.

"I have told you, I am not the Death Merchant," Camellion replied innocently.

Yubishkanonavitch quit smiling. "Look out your window, Death Merchant."

Camellion looked, and what he saw made him frown

with envy. A few hundred feet below, off to the left, a hundred-foot square of countryside was actually moving, sliding slowly to the left, revealing a well-lighted, ever-widening entrance below the surface of the frozen soil. Now the Death Merchant knew the score, knew why the chopper was landing on supposedly barren terrain. The helicopter was about to land in an underground hangar—*Damned clever of the pig farmers to construct an underground pig pen!*

To make sure the insult was properly rubbed in, Paul Yubishkanonavitch purred sarcastically, "As you can see, Death Merchant, we are not stupid. I say that because we know that you consider us nothing more than peasants. Your spy satellites can take all the photographs they want. Their cameras will photograph nothing but real trees and genuine ice and snow and rocks. There is no way your topography experts in NSA will be able to detect our underground installations. The heat sensors aboard your satellites are also useless. Our base is too far down."

Camellion did not answer. There wasn't anything he could say. Yubishkanonavitch was right.

He continued to watch as the huge square of land below—it was really the top of the hangar—moved slowly on its rails to one side, to its maximum. Yubishkanonavitch nodded to the pilot, who swung the helicopter to the left, centering it over the tremendous hole. Then the craft began its descent straight down, finally settling gently on the concrete pad fifty feet below the surface. The pilot switched off the turboshaft engine, and the big rotor blades came to a halt.

Captain Yubishkanonavitch pulled a Stechkin machine pistol and motioned with it at Camellion as the guards picked up the ends of the five chains.

"Hurry up! Get up and get out," Yubishkanonavitch snapped. "We have a schedule to keep."

Camellion did as he was told, knowing resistance would be stupid and totally useless. In his business one could go wrong in many different directions, but right in only one. So far, he had gone wrong in all directions!

Camellion and his captors moved from the helicopter, and while other KGB security agents and technicians in the hangar watched he was marched to a vehicle that made him think of a car on a roller coaster. There was a difference: this car was larger and had six rubber tires.

With one of the KGB guards doing the driving, and Camellion sandwiched between Captain Yubishkanonavitch and Paruir Lovaya, the electric-powered car headed east through a tunnel that had been blasted from solid rock and lined with aluminum sheeting, a tunnel that slanted downward.

The Death Merchant thought of Doctor Raya Dubanova, the woman scientist who was his contact at Zemlya II. Forget her! He'd never be able to contact her now. NSA would never learn her tremendous secret, although it was suspected it had to do with the earth's magnetic field. Scientists knew that the intensity of the magnetic field had dropped from .8 to .5 gauss over the last 2,500 years in western Europe. In Japan, it was .7 gauss in A.D. 300, and it was now .55 gauss. Scientists also knew that the reversals of the magnetic field were not random. The behavior was cyclical, the field going through zero and coming out the other side. Intensity drops before reversals which occurred on an average of every half a million years. Scientists were worried. Should the intensity of the magnetic field keep dropping at its present rate, the ionosphere would collapse. That would be the end of all radio reception, and cancer of the skin would increase a thousandfold.

There was another surprise in store for the Death Merchant when the electric car sped out of the tunnel, and he saw that they were in a tremendously huge area that had been hollowed out of solid rock on three sides. The fourth side faced the bleak Arctic Ocean. Thirty feet overhead was a solid granite ceiling, held up by massive concrete supports spaced every fifty feet or so. Camellion was impressed. It must have taken the pig farmers years to build such an underground hog pen, blasting it right out of the rock beneath the hills above.

Within the area were square prefabricated buildings —barracks, workshops, recreational centers, and storage houses. But what really caught Camellion's eye were the submarine pens jutting out into the sea. Yes sir, the damned Russians had been busy little bears all right. Wiese Island was more than a weather station, far more than part of a route that supplied Zemlya II. Wiese Island was also a submarine base. Five submarines were in the slips, three conventional diesel-powered types and two sleek nuclear subs of the giant Delta class.

The driver drove the electric car straight to the dock area, and Camellion saw that there were five other subs in the pens. He had not been able to see them from a distance because, being unconventional craft, the U-boats had no "sail," or conning towers.

Only ninety-six-feet long, not quite half the length of a World War II underseas boat (the German type VIIC variant was 220 feet long), these "passenger little-boats" reminded the Death Merchant of the US Navy's DSRV's—deep submergence rescue vehicles. Yet unlike Uncle Sam's DSRV's, these "little-boats" were true submarines. The proof was clearly there before the Death Merchant when he looked at one of the odd vessels, which as it lay in drydock, had the full length of its gray hull exposed. There were the diving planes, and an enormous propeller, at least five feet long, sticking out from the pointed stern. On the hull at the stern were twin rudders, one above and one below the prop, which was surrounded by a steel mesh guard.

Topside, about ten feet from the rounded bow, was a rounded "bump," a lock-wheel sticking up from the hatch-cover. Toward the center of the topside was a much smaller protuberance; there were two more small projections on the port side. Two on the starboard side, the side Camellion could not see? He wondered. There were no portholes, and no evidence of a periscope well mounting.

Captain Yubishkanonavitch and the KGB guards escorted the Death Merchant to a dock, pushed him across the gangplank to the open hatch of a "little-boat" and forced him down the ladder into the interior of the small submarine.

Three other Russians, all USSR naval officers, were already inside, and as soon as the KGB political security service guards were inside and the upper hatch locked, the "passenger little-boat" got underway, moving slowly out of the slip.

Captain Yubishkanonavitch sat down next to Camellion, who was watching the six television screens in front of the driver of the sub. The TV screens explained why the sub carried no periscope; they also explained the various small "bumps" on the hull of the vessel and why each bump had a lens in its center. The projections contained television cameras which transmitted the images to the television screens in front of the driver. All he had to do was check the screens to see what was in the water outside the vessel, off the bow, the port, the starboard, and the stern, as well as topside and below the keel.

The Death Merchant noted, too, that the Russian pilot steered the U-boat in much the same manner as one would fly an airplane, turning the wheel to either the left or the right for horizontal direction, and pulling it back or pushing it away for altitude or descent, in this case for either diving or surfacing.

For its small size, the submarine was roomy. Camellion estimated that half of the U-boat was reserved for human cargo, with the remaining half given to engine compartments, pumps, and ballast tanks. Camellion also realized that the source of power was electricity from batteries; the low, steady hum throughout the boat told him so.

Across the aisle from Camellion sat two of the Russian navy men and three of the security agents. The two other KGB guards sat on Camellion's left. To his right was Captain Yubishkanonavitch, who couldn't resist bragging about "superior" Russian marine technology.

"It will take us only a short while to make the journey to Zemlya II," he mocked. "These boats can do twenty knots on the surface and eleven and a half knots submerged. We have twenty of them which shuttle back and forth from Zemlya II to Sovietskaya Station I."

"Comrade Yubishkanonavitch, do you think it is wise to reveal such things to a foreign spy?" asked one of the Russian naval officers across from the Death Merchant. "There is such a thing as security, or have you forgotten, Comrade Yubishkanonavitch?"

"As a member of the KGB, I can assure you that I have not forgotten about security," snapped Yubishkanonavitch, his eyes as cruel as his voice as he glared at the navy officer. "I suggest, Lieutenant Blokady, that you do not intrude into matters which do not concern you."

Lieutenant Blokady, a young blond Russian, looked embarrassed, but he did not argue. Made of sterner stuff, Lieutenant Garthoff, his companion, stared right back at Yubishkanonavitch and spoke up.

"Should he be released from prison a few years from now and exchanged for one of our boys, what is to prevent him from telling his government what he has seen and heard? Have you considered that possibility, Comrade Yubishkanonavitch?"

For a moment Captain Yubishkanonavitch studied Lieutenant Garthoff; then he touched Camellion on the shoulder. "This man will never go to prison," he said firmly. "He will be executed. He's the Death Merchant. Do you think for a moment that Moscow is going to let him live?"

The eyes of the two Russian naval officers widened in disbelief. They stared at Camellion as though he were a Martian, but neither man said anything. The Death Merchant! One of the most dangerous enemies of the USSR!

The voyage continued in silence, with only the humming of the electric batteries and the occasional sound of the pumps connected to the ballast tanks. Watching the television screens, Camellion tried to find a solution to his predicament, his mind desperately searching for answers that would not come. Presently, in the bow television screen, he saw what had to be Zemlya II.

Watching Camellion, Yubishkanonavitch confirmed the sighting.

"Yes, that is Zemlya II," he boasted, "and don't

pretend that the United States has anything on the ocean's floor to match it!"

Camellion continued to watch the television screen, much to the consternation of the two Russian naval officers, who would have preferred to have had him blindfolded.

Zemlya II was an incredible sight. As the submarine drew closer, Camellion could see the underwater city in all its eerie splendor. Stretched out in a row were five transparent domes, each dome almost half a city block in diameter, each dome connected to its neighbor by a transparent tube. Camellion judged that the height of each dome, at its apex, was between sixty-five and seventy-five feet, and that the connecting tubes were about fifty feet long and twenty feet in diameter. Just as remarkable were the prefabricated buildings within the domes. Some of these were two stories tall. In the soft glow of sodium-vapor lights, the buildings sparkled with a pale sheen, as though the material of which they were composed was either of polished stone or shiny metal.

Reality can often be staggering in its implications! The Death Merchant realized that what he was looking at was an impossibility—at least in theory! Modern science had not advanced to the point that it could build such a complex under water. Whether the domes were of glass or plastic, their size and shape could not be any protection against the tremendous pressure of the water pushing at every square inch of their surfaces. At this depth of 1,200 feet, the water should have flattened the domes the way a brick would smash an air-filled cellophane bag. But such was not the case with Zemlya II. There could be only one explanation: either the domes were of a material that was neither glass nor plastic, or else Russian scientists had discovered a revolutionary new process involving pressurization.

Taking advantage of Yubishkanonavitch's boastful nature, the Death Merchant went on a fishing expedition.

"I don't believe it,'" Camellion said. He turned and looked at Yubishkanonavitch. "I think Zemlya

II is nothing but an illusion. I think you've put a phony image on the screen. There's no transparent material on earth that could withstand such pressure. If you tell me the domes are plastic or glass, I'll have to call you a liar!"

Captain Yubishkanonavitch didn't try to conceal his surprise. The two navy officers looked both relieved and amused. The KGB guards smiled.

"The domes are not glass or plastic," Yubishkanonavitch said matter-of-factly. "I don't know what they're made of. I can assure you, however, that Zemlya II is not an illusion. One cannot enter an illusion as we soon will be doing."

With a loud sigh, Camellion shifted his weight slightly, the movement rattling his chains.

"I suppose that anything man can conceive, man can eventually do, or build," Camellion said, "no matter how fantastic the concept."

"Undoubtedly," Yubishkanonavitch said. "There are exceptions. Even our brilliant scientists must admit the impossibility of a four-sided triangle."

"Which only goes to prove how far behind the times you Russians are," Camellion said, "or you'd know that the Egyptians knew about a four-sided triangle more than five thousand years ago!"

"That's a lie!" one of the KGB agents, across from Camellion, snapped. Murdering Camellion with his eyes, the man hunched forward, his arms folded across his chest. "There can be no four-sided triangle. Even a capitalist pig like you should know that. The stupid Egyptians could not have discovered that which cannot be!"

Camellion derived a savage delight from making the man appear stupid in front of his comrades.

"No? Then what would you call a three-dimensional pyramid, if not a four-sided triangle?" The Death Merchant smiled in malicious enjoyment. "I should think you pig farmers would be the first to understand that. Didn't you invent mathematics? According to Moscow, the Russians have always been first in everything!"

The KGB man muttered some low expletives under his breath and averted his eyes. The rest of the Russians seemed embarrassed, all except Captain Yubishkanona-vitch, who didn't seem at all disturbed by Camellion's having turned the tables on the KGB agent, making the man appear stupid. Yubishkanonavitch found that he could not be truly angry with a man he considered a corpse! At best, the *Amerikanski* had only a few months of life left to him.

"A second before the bullets from the rifles of the execution squad strike your body, you can reflect that it was the Egyptians who built the pyramids," Yubishka-nonavitch said, his voice slightly contemptuous, "and remember how you were inside Zemlya II, the only true underwater city in the world."

One of the KGB agents, who was sitting to Camellion's left, leaned out, turned his head, and looked at both the Death Merchant and Yubishkanonavitch. "This bourgeois bastard shouldn't mind dying," the man jeered, taunting Camellion with his eyes. "He comes from a Christian country. Surely he has lived a good and clean life."

"Yes, that is true," Camellion said solemnly in reply. "I was a living saint. Just the same, I'd like to live a little longer to dirty it up a bit. I think I'll do just that, live to a ripe old age." He winked at the KGB agent who was staring at him in puzzlement.

"General Vershensky will disagree with those plans." Yubishkanonavitch said, his tone low and vicious. "He is in charge of security within the domes and hates foreign agents. You'll be standing before him within the hour."

The Death Merchant, ignoring Yubishkanonavitch, directed his attention at the television screens, his lean face reflecting an intensely frowning concentration, a thinly disguised anger barely under control—the face of a man for whom failure was unthinkable. It was not the face of a man who expected to die.

The submarine was so close to the domes of Zemlya II that Camellion could distinguish numerous details. For example, he now saw that the sodium-vapor lights were not mounted to the corners of the buildings as he had previously thought; instead, the light tubes were fastened to the ceilings of the domes.

Now, too, it was possible for the Death Merchant to distinguish various kinds of installations and equipment outside the domes. Clustered around the five giant domes were smaller transparent spheres, so tiny that, in comparison, the spheres resembled pinheads floating around a basketball.

These ten-foot translucent spheres, mounted in frames anchored to the ocean's bottom, were pressurized sub-igloos—outside two-man stations where personnel from Zemlya II could rest while outside the domes and recirculate the air in their breathing units. The sub-igloos were used for any number of reasons—not only as rest stops but as guard stations as well.

Several hundred feet to the left of the last dome on the television screen, the Death Merchant could see a "sea spider," its twenty-foot aluminum float tethered to the bottom by four-hundred-and-fifty-foot steel legs. The sea spider was an underwater weather station. The instruments inside the float measured the strength and force of the water and transmitted the data to Zemlya II. Current meters and a buoy with an anemometer, floating on the surface, yet still fastened to the spider, measured waves and wind.

Reluctantly, Camellion was forced to conclude that the Soviets were far in advance of Uncle Sam in the exploration of the oceans. More proof lay in the wave-power generating station a short distance to the side of the first dome. A large metal vane, fifty feet high and five hundred feet long, was attached to an axle, which in turn was attached to a pump. Underwater waves striking the vane caused the vane to turn the axle; it was the moving axle that activated the pump, and the power of the pumped water—thousands of gallons a minute—was used to operate three huge generators in the control dome of Zemlya II.

"We will dock very shortly," Comrade Yubishkanonavitch said to Camellion, his low voice ringing with pride.

"I rather surmised that we would," Camellion said somberly. He transferred his gaze to the KGB officer and gave him a long, searching look. "How do we do it?

Swim from here to there? I don't see any lock-out chamber on this baby!"

"We do not have one," Yubishkanonavitch said in a low voice. "The lock-out chamber is in the control dome. Keep watching the screen and soon you will see it for yourself."

Camellion hoped his face didn't register the rage possessing him, the naked fury originally fueled by his capture and now intensified by his having to admit the superiority of Soviet underwater technology. Just think of it, an l.o.c. within the control dome itself, large enough to handle even a small submarine! Life was full of surprises, sad and bitter surprises.

Divers used a lock-out chamber—a compartment that could be pressurized to match surrounding water—as a doorway, as an entrance to and from the ocean. Lock-out chambers were common the world over, but not of a size that would hold a submarine. One of such proportions had never been needed—not in the West. To the Death Merchant, the fact that the Soviets had such a chamber was more evidence of how far Russian scientists had progressed in the exploration of the oceans. Yet pressurizing an l.o.c. was small potatoes compared to pressurizing the five gigantic domes. Camellion was no scientist; nevertheless, he knew enough about the process of pressurization to know that at this depth there was no known system that could hold back millions of tons of water exerting hundreds of pounds pressure per square inch. Taking into consideration the size of each dome, the combined pressure against each dome had to be hundreds of millions of pounds. Damn it, the Soviets had to be employing new pressurization techniques!

The Death Merchant and the Russians had to hold on to their seats as the pilot turned the sub sharply to starboard and prepared to swing the craft toward the front of the first dome, the control dome. It was a maneuver that put the boat three hundred feet to the left of the dome and a hundred feet above its center and permitted the men to catch sight of the lock-out chamber, the keel and starboard cameras picking up the images.

In spite of his determination to appear unimpressed, Camellion inhaled audibly with surprise, his visible shock giving Captain Yubishkanonavitch a warm feeling of satisfaction.

The Death Merchant stared at the two television screens in disbelief. The l.o.c. was an entire dock area filled with a couple of dozen long slips, many of them large enough to contain nuclear submarines. During those few moments, Camellion estimated that the lock occupied almost a fourth of the entire dome, a transparent wall separating the superpressurized lock from the rest of the complex.

The submarine made a wide half-circle to starboard. The pilot pushed forward on the control-column, sending the sub down toward the mouth of the sixty-foot diameter tube. Situated at a point where the bottom edge of the dome met the floor of the ocean, the entrance grew larger and larger as the sub approached it. Then the sub entered and was moving through the tube. From its sides glowed sodium-vapor lights.

The Death Merchant had arrived at Zemlya II!

He wouldn't have planned it this way—

But I made it! I'm here!

Chapter Four

Rostislav Pavlovich Vershensky's affable manner had not fooled Richard Camellion. The more the Death Merchant analyzed the behavior of the KGB general, who looked like a big shambling bear you felt like giving a cookie to, the more he was convinced that Vershensky was an extremely clever man. Then again, a KGB general had to be, in order to survive and to remain on top in the cutthroat labyrinth which was the Soviet secret police. The difference was that Vershensky was smarter than most Communist bureaucrats. An old Bolshevik who had survived the Stalin purges and had cunningly maneuvered his way through the Khrushchev era, Vershensky was a gray fox who could sense personal danger the way a master chess player can detect in advance the next six moves of his opponent—an old fox and a master hunter!

For twenty-seven years, Vershensky had been a policeman, his blood-stained career beginning in the Soviet military intelligence. In 1938 he had transferred to the KGB. when that infamous organization was still called the People's Commissariat for Internal Affairs. And he had survived! He had stayed alive and had prospered because he was not only a genius at survival, he was a master manipulator who instinctively stayed on the safe side of the right people, the people in power. Steadily, over the years, he had advanced in rank. Now he had reached the top and was a full General in the KGB's Political Security Service.

During the previous half-hour the Death Merchant had arrived at the conclusion that with Vershensky he had a choice between cholera and the plague. Oddly enough, Vershensky had not used the usual KGB interrogation tactics. He hadn't even used veiled threats. Instead, he had immediately taken an attitude that was almost conciliatory, if not downright friendly. Indeed, one might have thought that Camellion was an honored guest! But the whole act was a waste of time. The Death Merchant wasn't impressed nor surprised by this part of the KGB softening-up process. In fact, General Vershensky's counterfeit friendliness only proved to the Death Merchant that the KGB boss was underestimating him. Sure, that was par for the course. A feeling of superiority, born of a deeply rooted sense of inferiority, had always been the Achilles Heel of pig farmers in general and the KGB in particular.

In a way, thought Camellion, it was all rather amusing, like a game—a very deadly game in which the loser had no choice but to join the ranks of the doomed, the damned, and the dead.

Yeah . . . as funny as the hidden hinges of hell in a hideous sort of way. While General Vershensky continued to talk and act like a fat-faced Ukrainian farmer welcoming his guest, the other Russians in the control dome's central control room watched Camellion with undisguised suspicion in their eyes. The exceptions were Comrade Yubishkanonavitch and the five agents from the *Mikhail Lomonosov*. By now, Yubishkanonavitch and his agents were convinced that the incredible Death Merchant was only a mortal man like themselves. Such was not the case with General Vershensky's Zemlya officers and three scientists who were also in the control room.

The way the Russians were grouped around him, Camellion felt like a gladiator in a Roman amphitheater. In front of him sat jolly old Vershensky, who didn't look like any Jolly Green Giant. In his neat deep blue uniform with red accoutrements, Vershensky looked like what he was: a scheming and calculating Soviet autocrat.

Richard Camellion sat on a straight-back chair, seven feet in front of the desk. To his right, their eyes never wavering from him, were Vershensky's three stooges, Colonel Pyotr Wrangel, Major Ivan Sedin, and Captain Vasily Tur. Bucolic and menacing, well-built, well-fed sadists in their forties, the three KGB officers would have liked to see Camellion torn limb from limb; if they could have had their way, he would have been.

To the Death Merchant's left were Doctor Josef Krasnoyarsk, a geologist and seismologist who was an authority on tsunamis phenomena, the study of seismic tidal waves; Doctor Sergei Tikhon, a marine biologist from the Lenin Institute in Moscow; and Doctor Lexi Borsilinskow, who was one of the world's leading oceanographers.

The slim, waspish-looking Borsilinskow was to the Soviet Union what Doctor Kevin Black (of the Woods Hole Oceanographic Institute) was to the United States. In charge of the 270 scientists and technicians at Zemlya II, Borsilinskow shared command of the underwater installation with General Vershensky, who was in charge of all security.

Staring at Camellion as though they expected him to explode and kill them all, the three scientists didn't know what to make of the Death Merchant. From the stories they had heard over the years, their orderly minds could arrive at only one conclusion. No sane man could have accomplished what he was rumored to have done! Therefore, the Death Merchant was crazy!

To the rear of Camellion was Captain Paul Yubishkanonavitch and his agents, watching every move the Death Merchant made. Three of the agents held machine pistols in their laps, the weapons half hidden by their uniform caps. Not that the Death Merchant was doing handsprings! But General Vershensky had ordered the dog chains removed from his wrists, ankles, and neck, and Yubishkanonavitch and his men were taking no chances.

General Vershensky folded his big hands on the desk and smiled graciously. "The first chief directorate was very delighted to hear about your capture, Camellion," he said politely, "especially Special Service II, and Vershensky laughed loudly as if enjoying an enormous joke. "I am assuming that you know Special Service II is our counterintelligence and that Department-V consists of our 'wet affairs' people."

"Seems like I've heard of those departments," Camellion said dryly, his face carefully deadpan. "Or maybe I read about them in *Reader's Digest*. That's an American magazine."

The Death Merchant, catching Vershensky's piercing gaze, stared straight at the KGB general. These Russians! They were so wholeheartedly naive about their deceitfulness. That is why the Russians were such liars and idle talkers, and why they never tried to justify their behavior—because they didn't have any social principles, or know of any from which they could choose. They were always willing to lie and babble and brag because they had no conscience. Yet they were always patient, having learned to be so as a necessity, because of their usually violent tempers.

Suspicion was another trait with which the Russians were burdened—perhaps their most prominent trait. Indeed, few people could be more mistrustful than the Russians, whose inherent fear of strangers had been intensified by their revolutionary experience—another reason why Camellion wanted to laugh at General Vershensky's absurd pretense at friendliness and easy sociability. Such a tactic was even an insult to Camellion's intelligence—*Or is that idiot so dumb that he can't realize I know the pig farmers as well as I know the Americans?*

Paradoxically, Russians were always polite with strangers—watchful, mistrustful, but still polite. When officials or members of the Party addressed each other, they always used the word "comrade." However, "comrade" was often used by the average Russian, since it was also the equivalent of "Mr." But when addressing foreigners from capitalist countries, "gentleman" was the word of choice. When speaking to Russian civilians, officials employed the form of address meaning "citizen."

Just to confuse General Vershensky, the Death Merchant added, "As I remember, each time I tangled with agents from Special Service II or Department-V, your boys lost. And I am assuming that you know of those KGB losses, General. It wasn't anything personal. They had their job to do, and I had mine."

"Of course, of course," Vershensky agreed cordially, a funny look flashing across his broad peasant's face. "As you Americans are fond of saying, 'win a few, lose a few.' Another truth is that it's the final battle that counts. It is that battle you have lost, Gentleman Camellion. You're our prisoner, and there is no possibility of your escaping." Vershensky paused for a moment, then his manner became very confidential. "One of our nuclear submarines will be docking here at Zemlya II in a few days. It will take you to Leningrad. From Leningrad you will be flown to Moscow." A triumphant gleam appeared on his face. "And since you admit to killing KGB agents, am I to understand that you admit being the Death Merchant?"

"All the attention I've been getting, it would seem I'm considered a prize by the KGB chairman and his chief directorates." Camellion's voice was jovial. "I'd think Andropov and his 'yes men' would want to fly me to Moscow as quickly as possible."

"General Vershensky asked you a question, you impertinent dog!" Colonel Pyotr Wrangel said loudly, his knife-edged countenance darkening in hate. "Do you admit being the Death Merchant? You murderous as-sassin! Moscow will get the truth out of you!"

"And so would we, in short order, if Moscow hadn't ordered hands off," Major Ivan Sedin sneered. "They want us to save you for them. They want you fresh and healthy when they go to work on you."

"That's enough, Comrades," General Vershensky said. "We do not want Gentleman Camellion to think we use inhumane methods in forcing the enemies of the state to reveal their crimes against the Soviet people." He smiled paternally at the stone-faced Camellion. "We have more advanced ways of extracting information from our enemies."

"I can imagine!" Camellion snorted. He stretched out his legs, raised his arms, and locked his fingers behind his head. "Even when your own people disagree with the system, they're put in so called 'insane asylums' and brain-washed! Or if they're people who've invoked world sympathy, such as Solzhenitsyn, your government boots them out of the country. That's Soviet 'justice' for you!"

"Solzhenitsyn! That damned bourgeois type!" growled Captain Vasily Tur. "That enemy of the people should have received a life sentence in the Gulag!"

"Yes, I'm the Death Merchant," Camellion went on, "and while you have me now, there isn't anything you can do about my past successes. I stopped Russian total-itarianism in Cuba, in the Middle East, and in a lot of other places—and I'm damned proud of it!"

In admitting that he was the Death Merchant, Camel-lion had decided to tell the truth. Why bother to deny what the KGB already knew? Besides, Camellion reason-ed, his problem did not revolve around his identity. Escape: that was his only goal.

I either escape or die! It was that simple, and at this stage of the game—impossible!

Colonel Wrangel seemed pleased with himself, think-ing that it had been he who had gotten Camellion to admit he was the Death Merchant. Major Sedin and Captain Tur looked surprised. Not so with General Ver-shensky. With his mouth in a half-smile and with a measured look in his cornflower blue eyes, he removed

53

a cigarette from a pack on his desk and carefully inserted it into a small red holder, all the while giving Camellion quick, darting glances.

"Getting back to what you said about being a 'prize'— Yes, Chairman Andropov considers you the prize catch of the year," Vershensky said. "He does want you to be brought to Moscow as soon as possible. It's the Arctic weather that prevented our flying you from Sovietskaya I. You are too valuable a prize to risk on the terrible winter weather. Much safer to use a submarine."

The KGB general stopped talking, clicked on a desk lighter, and touched the flame to the end of the cigarette. Then he said slyly, "Since you have admitted being the Death Merchant, why not make it easier on yourself and tell us how the Central Intelligence Agency discovered Zemlya II. Moscow—"

"I never said I was working for the CIA," Camellion said, deliberately yawning to annoy the Three Stooges, as well as Yubishkanonavitch and the other KGB gorillas.

"Sooner or later you will have to tell the truth," persisted Vershensky. "The interrogators in Moscow can be most persuasive. Come now, you're a professional. You know the reality of the situation. You're far too intelligent to believe you can hold out against our people at headquarters. They will eventually get the full truth from you."

"Uh huh, with the 'advanced methods,' as you earlier referred to them. With aversion therapy. I believe that's what the KGB calls its methods. It's one of those clean scientific terms, like electrophysiology, chemotherapy, or psychosurgery—which really mean mind control, the conditioning of a human being to confess, or to behave out of fear. Come off of it, General! Whom do you think you're kidding? Even the North Koreans took lessons from you pig farmers, and those slant-eyed lice are no amateurs in the field of mind-breaking!"

General Vershensky shrugged. For a moment he looked thoughtfully at the end of his cigarette, then his eyes shot to the Death Merchant.

"Why complain, Camellion?" he said. "Why accuse us of cruelty when your own people use the same identical methods? We of the KGB are not fools. We read your news magazines, and all your so-called 'liberal' publications. We know that aversion therapy is widely practiced in the United States prison systems. The *Amerkanskis* have even tried its use with problem children. 'Behavior modification' is the term your government officials use; yet no matter what Washington calls it, it is still behaviorism, which rightly denies man's consciousness and teaches that he's merely the highest of all animals, that he is only a series of responses conditioned by his environment. In that respect, your science is fifty years behind the glorious science of our Communist society. For over fifty years we have known that man is nothing more than a machine to be molded for the good of society. Our own Ivan Petrovich Pavlov proved it when he caused his dogs to salivate at the sound of a bell."

Richard Camellion made an insulting sound with his mouth. He hated to admit, even to himself, that General Vershensky was right. Aversion therapy was being widely practiced in the United States.

He ridiculed the Russian general, using a Russian idiom that meant "to throw dust in my face." Its equivalent in English would be "You're pulling my leg." Not wanting to look foolish in front of the Soviets, Camellion could only hope that Vershensky didn't have all the facts.

General Vershensky didn't laugh. Instead, he grew serious as he carefully placed his cigarette in its holder (somehow the holder looked familiar to Camellion) in the slot of an ashtray, pulled open a drawer of his desk, and took out a thick brown folder.

"It's a remarkable coincidence," he said, opening the expanding file, "but only a week ago, these reports arrived from headquarters in Moscow. They were sent in order that our men stationed here could keep informed of events in the United States."

Vershensky took a thick packet of papers from the file and placed the folder next to the dozen photographs which the KGB had taken of Camellion on board the *Mikhail Lomonosov*. He next looked at the top paper in his hands and glanced at Camellion.

"This is about a booklet that our embassy in Washington, D. C., bought through the United States Govern-

55

ment Printing Office," Vershensky said. "The report"—
he looked at the paper—"is entitled 'Individual
Rights and the Federal Role in Behavior Modification.'
The report—it was compiled by one of your US Senators
named Sam Ervin—tells of prisoners forced to become
experimental guinea pigs, and all kinds of group therapy
similar to North Korean brainwashing. The report tells
of a company in your state of Nebraska which specializes
in shock treatment apparatus. Not only that, Camellion,
the report clearly describes the role the US Departments
of Health, Education and Welfare, Labor, Justice, and
Defense played in such therapy. The Veterans Administration, Law Enforcement Assistance Administration,
and the National Science Foundation were also involved."

Vershensky looked up from the paper, a frown on his
ruddy forehead. His cold eyes bored into Camellion.
"I will now read, word for word, exerpts from an article
that appeared in a magazine named *Argosy*. The following is from the November, 1975, issue.

" 'Dr. Arnold A. Hutchnecker is a wizened, diminutive
man who, at 76, still practices psychiatry in a spacious
Park Avenue office on New York's upper east side. In
1951, some 15 years after his emigration from Hitler's
Germany, "Hutschie," as he is called by intimates, was
paid a visit by an aspiring young Senator named Richard
Nixon. As Vice-President, Nixon continued to drop by
over the next few years, once after what the doctor has
described as a very rough trip overseas. Advised that the
visits were unsound politically, Nixon stopped coming
for a time. But according to the late columnist Drew
Pearson, he was seen entering Hutschnecker's building
throughout the 1960s. The doctor himself has acknow-
ledged ongoing "social calls."

"In 1965, at his friend Nixon's suggestion, Gerald
Ford also began seeing——' "

"Get to the point, General!" Camellion interrupted.
"Even presidents and vice-presidents can have emotional
problems."

General Vershensky looked up at Camellion and smiled thinly.

"Very well, I shall get to the point." He looked down at the second sheet and began to read:

" 'But consider a Hutschnecker proposal, first outlined in a 1970 memo to Nixon's White House, which proposed mass psychological testing of all six-to-eight-year-olds "to detect the children who have violent and homicidal tendencies." On a compulsory basis, those who were found to be "severely disturbed" would then be assigned to "camps with group activities." There they they would learn "more socially acceptable behavior patterns.' "

The Death Merchant shifted uncomfortably on his chair. "The plan was never implemented. The American people wouldn't have stood for it."

"Oh no!" exclaimed Vershensky, sounding as if he were congratulating himself. "Let me quote the following from the same article in the magazine known as *Argosy*." His eyes flashed down to the page, and he began to read.

" 'Yet Hutschnecker's basic formula is now coming to pass. The Ervin Report discloses a California program, "not yet fully confirmed," to computerize files on "pre-delinquent" children so that early behavior problems can be watched and "the individuals who exhibit these tendencies can be checked for the rest of their lives." Prepared without consent of the parents, these files are linked up to those of various law enforcement agencies.' "

Haughtily, Vershensky looked up at Camellion, who stared straight back at him.

"There is more, Gentleman Camellion. I quote directly: 'The fact remains that Hutschnecker's plan is not unlike one proposed in Nazi Germany. A 1943 memo of the Gestapo's Crimino-Biological Institute suggests: 'The task is to identify as early as possible the criminally inclined person. Those with continual character failures who are fully capable of work will be put into a youth protection camp.' "

Vershensky, finished with the page, put it on the bottom of the pile, and again stared at the Death Merchant, his face total arrogance.

"Now deny that your fascist government isn't using Nazi methods," he said softly, "and don't tell me that this article in the *Argosy* magazine is a lie. You *Ameri-kanskis* have strict libel laws, and I'm sure the editors of the magazine verified the story before they would permit it to be printed."

He looked down at the page before him, the one on top of the stack. "Listen to this. Again, I quote directly. 'The making of an automaton, a Frankenstein-like "terminal man" is now scarcely a scalpel's length away. Already from the Harvard laboratory of Doctor Ralph Schwitzgebel, a Behavior Transmitter-Reinforcer carried on a belt allows tracking and a wearer's location, transmits information about his activities, and communicates with him by tone signals.'

" 'A report appearing in *Issues of Criminology*—"The Use of Electronics in the Observation and Control of Human Behavior and its Possible Use in Rehabilitation and Parole"—takes Schwitzgebel's creation one step beyond. It tells of a radio-telemetric system now on the drawing board, consisting of an implanted tiny transmitter with a battery-powered oscillator, which probes deep into the subcortical regions of a man's brain and sends codes to a police computer that monitors bodily changes.'

" 'Funded by HEW'—that's your government's Department of Health, Education and Welfare, Mr. Camellion—'the National Center for the Study of Crime and Delinquency lists 19 projects in schools, mental institutions and prisons on "developing methods to control abnormal attitudes." These include experiments on electrical stimulation of the brain to curb violence at Maryland's Patuxent Institution . . . .' "

General Vershensky smiled like a cherub at Camellion, straightened the batch of papers in his hands by tapping their bottom edges on the desk, and returned them to the expanding folder. After he tied the ribbon around the folder, he returned the file to the desk's drawer, and, from the same drawer, removed a large 8" × 11" envelope into which he put Camellion's photographs and two fingerprint cards. Carefully, he closed the flap of the envelope, bent down the metal sealers, and put the envelope into the same drawer that held the folder containing the photostats on United States mind-control experiments.

By now, the cigarette in the ashtray had burned itself out. As General Vershensky took another cigarette from the pack and inserted it into the small red holder, he continued to give Camellion ruminative glances, as if trying to pierce Camellion's persona and snatch his real thoughts from the vault of his mind.

With his arms folded over his chest, Richard was fantasizing how nice it would be if he could get his hands on the Three Stooges, who were smirking at him, their taunting expressions transmitting their challenge to him, daring him to refute General Vershensky's accusations against the US Government.

The fact that he couldn't made the Death Merchant all the more angry. The damned pig farmer general had been right! Uncle Sam was experimenting with behavior modification. Uncle Sam was up to his 200-year-old beard in experiments that, years before, had first been suggested in Nazi Germany. And why not? With any nation, the name of the game was survival! Already the United States was a second-rate nation, and if crime continued to rise, if government continued to favor big business while millions of old people went to bed hungry every night . . . if, if, if—then the US would damn soon be a third-rate nation. None of which was Camellion's concern! A realist, he was convinced that if his mind ceased to exist, the concept which he called the world, so far as he knew, would cease to exist, too. Yeah! Absolute is a meaningless diagram, a superfluous complication of nonsense! *Reductio ad absurdum!* Philosophy and do-goodism belonged to the mystics and the masochists (both were kissin' cousins). A practical man built his world around the universe of his own interests. He did what he wanted to do—or at least tried to—and didn't waste time and energy worrying about things he couldn't change. Yeah, if Uncle Sam wanted to try for a police state, that was Sam's business.

General Vershensky let smoke curl lazily from his nose, leaned back in his swivel chair, and crossed his legs, his stare still speculative, his gaze continuing to imprison Camellion while he wondered how any human being could keep his face expressionless for so lengthy a period.

Finally Vershensky said, "Yes, Gentleman Camellion. We both must admit that all governments are interested in only one thing: the sweet fruits that fall from the tree of power. Your government thinks it has the right to cover this planet with a blanket of decadence called democracy. We in turn feel that it is our mission to extend Communism over the face of the earth. The dialectics of our system prove we will eventually succeed. Unlike capitalism, Communism does not contain the seeds of its own destruction. That is why there must be revolutionary violence—violence for the eventual good of humanity!"

"Well spoken, Comrade General Vershensky!" Major Sedin spoke up. "As Lenin stressed, 'The replacement of the bourgeois by the proletarian state is impossible without a violent revolution!'"

The Death Merchant slapped the major with laughing eyes. "Tell me, Major. What is the price of brass bananas in Moscow?"

Major Sedin blinked in confusion at the Death Merchant. He opened his mouth, then closed it again.

Colonel Wrangel leaned close to Sedin and whispered in his ear, "He's throwing dust in your face and trying to make you look foolish."

Major Sedin froze, his quick embarrassment changing to instant anger, which expressed itself in flushed cheeks and a penetrating stare. If a single look could have killed, the Death Merchant would have disintegrated instantly.

The Death Merchant gave Vershensky the benefit of his attention.

"I know all your Commie clichés, General," he said. "Like, 'Force is the midwife of every old society pregnant with a new one!' Unquote Karl Heinrich Marx. And in case you and your stooges don't know it, he was a Jew—who descended from a long line of rabbis. The paradox is that he was a ferocious anti-Semite. If he had lived under Hitler, he probably would have been a Nazi. He was also profoundly Slavophobic and definitely anti-Russian. Put that in your samovar and boil it!"

"That's a damned imperialist lie!" Captain Vasily

Tur said angrily. "Marx was anti-Semite, but he loved the Slavic peoples!"

Tur became even more infuriated when Camellion ignored him.

"Marx did have a lot stupid theories, but now and then he did say something that made sense," Camellion said. "Quote, 'Religion is the opiate of the people!' unquote. At least he had the sense to recognize the tyranny of priestcraft in all its forms."

General Vershensky's roughhewn face brightened. "We have known for quite a few years that you are an atheist, such as ourselves."

"You're wrong, General," Camellion said. "I'm not an atheist—not that it makes any difference. One man's religion can be another man's hell." Once again he put his hands behind his head, leaned back on the chair, and stretched out his legs. "I'm the prisoner of the KGB. That's a fact. Soon I'll be in Moscow, and the center will give me 'the treatment.' Then, bang, bang! I'll be shot and nonexistent. Those, too, are facts. But I'm not complaining. Sooner or later, a mission had to fail. It was inevitable that I'd have to draw the black ace. Win a lot, but lose only one—eh, General?"

"Don't be so pessimistic, Mr. Camellion," Vershensky said soothingly. "Worry is nothing more than today's mouse eating tomorrow's cheese. Your predicament may not be as serious as you think it is."

"Praise the Lord!" mocked Camellion, harsh edges of strain revealed in his voice and in his tight face. "So tell me what's worse than being dead!"

"Comrade Director Andropov and his associates at the center in Moscow aren't unreasonable men," Vershensky said encouragingly. "Should you give them your full cooperation, who knows how your fortunes could change? Think about it, Death Merchant."

"You're saying a choice between life imprisonment in a Gulag—a labor camp—and being shot!" Camellion cracked. "That's not really a choice. I'd rather be shot ten times over!"

The joke was still on the Russians in that the Death Merchant wasn't at all concerned about standing in front of a firing squad. He would never give the swine tenders the pleasure of pumping him full of slugs. He'd take his own life if it came to that.

On board the *Mikhail Lomonosov* the KGB agents had gone over every square inch of his body, checking each scar and mole to see if they were phony. Experts that the agents were, they still had not found the two secret caches of poison on Camellion's body. They had discovered the artificial scar on Camellion's chest, just as he had hoped they would. They had soaked the two inch strip of plastisheen in hot water and then had injected the solution into one of the ship's cats. The poor animal had promply rolled over and died.

No, Comrade General Vershensky, I will never stand in front of a pig farmer firing squad, Camellion thought again. He watched as the Russian pulled open a drawer and took out a square bottle of vodka which he placed on top of the desk.

"Death or the Gulag!" he said easily. "But that is not necessarily what has to happen. Oh, no! Not at all." He continued to talk, his voice dripping with overtones of patronization, as he took two waterglasses from the drawer and placed them next to the bottle of vodka. "Comrade Director Andropov and his people are people of principle, people of understanding."

He continued to talk as he uncapped the bottle and filled the two glasses with vodka. "Until your capture, you were the Soviet Union's most dangerous enemy, but that does not mean that the center wants revenge. We Communists are beyond such self-defeating emotions. Comrade Director Andropov and the other people at the Center are practical and most pragmatic. I can assure you that they realize that as an American intelligence agent, you were only doing your duty by your country. Why, it is even possible that the special council group which deals with foreign agents will decide not to have you executed. You are a very talented man, and we Communists do not believe in waste. Of course, much will depend on you, Camellion . . . very much . . ."

Pretending to take the bait by lifting his eyes in pseudointerest, the Death Merchant congratulated himself. He had been right about Vershensky. *Like all Russians, the pig lover is so treacherous that he assumes*

I might be willing to sell out my country in exchange for life—or worse, that I might be willing to become a double agent! No way, you stupid Communist son of a bitch. Then again, it could all be a trick to get me to tell what I know about American intelligence. Either way, these Slavic sows are in for a surprise.

"Hmmmmm," Camellion mused, rubbing the end of his chin with thumb and forefinger, "patriotism would be a useless virtue to a dead man, wouldn't it?"

"Indeed it would," Vershensky agreed exuberantly and made a come-here motion to Camellion with one hand. "Come, have a drink! I have much work to do and won't be seeing you again before you are taken to Leningrad. Is there anything I can do for you during your short stay with us?"

Annoyed, Vershensky waved back Captain Yubish-kanonavitch and the other KGB guards who stepped forward as Camellion got up from the chair and moved over to the desk.

"Idiots! There is no place for him to run to," Vershensky spoke as if trying to pound down each word with a hammer, his eyes flashing like railroad-crossing signals. "Quit trying to impress me with your efficiency!"

"Comrade General Vershensky, this Death Merchant is a very dangerous imperialist spy!" Captain Yubish-kanonavitch said stiffly.

"Yes, I know. Too bad you and your men did not show some of that efficiency on the *Mikhail Lomonosov!* If you had, Comrade Captain Paul Yubishkanonavitch, a lot of KGB men would still be alive."

General Vershensky picked up his glass from the desk and smiled evilly, while Yubishkanonavitch and the guards stepped back awkwardly, their faces as expressionless as marble. To a man, they despised General Vershensky and his assistants at Zemlya II. Nonetheless, they never said anything derogatory about him, not even among themselves, fearing that one of their number might be an internal informer for the center in Moscow.

Camellion reached for the glass of vodka on the desk, and instantly, when he saw the card of cigarette holders next to the bottle, realization flooded his mind. Damn! What a small, small world!

General Vershensky, spotting the look of recognition on Camellion's face, glanced curiously at him. "Something is the matter?"

Camellion stretched a hand toward the card. "May I?"

Puzzled, Vershensky nodded. Richard picked up the card and looked at the red cigarette holders underneath the plastic window. The company's name and address were at the bottom of the card—*Venuri, Inc. 1610 Rollins Road. P.O. BOX1757. Burlingame, California, 94010.*

Now Camellion knew why Vershensky's holder had looked familiar to him! The card was filled with Tar Gard holders, the same kind of superfilters that Vallie West used!

"These holders," Camellion said thoughtfully, putting the card back down on the desk, "they remind me of a friend, that's all."

Vershensky nodded understandingly. "Ah, Gentleman Camellion, would your friend's name be Vallie West?" And when he saw the quick flash of surprise on the Death Merchant's face, he added slyly, "Yes, we know quite a bit about Vallie West, including his use of the amazing device known as Tar Gard. I understand the device is sold in drug stores all over your United States. I find that amazing. Our Embassy in Washington, D.C., buys them. But enough of this small talk. Time grows short."

He lifted his glass of vodka out to the Death Merchant.

"To your health!" he said, waiting and smiling, then frowning as Camellion lifted his glass and replied, "To your health, General—and to the sweet whispers of the dead!"

Camellion drank the vodka in one long swallow, the liquid burning his throat. General Vershensky downed his glass in one experienced gulp, wondering if he had impressed Camellion in any way. How could one tell what a capitalist dog like Camellion might be thinking? Such a man could kill with all the efficiency of a well-oiled machine and yet be able to comfort a nun or a small child. Well, let Comrade Director Andropov at the center deal with him. Andropov! That kiss-ass! The Death Merchant's capture would certainly increase Andropov's prestige with the Presidium. Comrade Chairman Brezhnev himself would probably congratulate him and give him a medal.

Vershensky put down his glass, sat down, and again flashed a phony smile at Camellion who had resumed sitting on the chair in front of the desk.

Dr. Lexi Borsilinskow spoke up, his voice surprisingly strong for a man who was a bantam-weight. "Comrade General Vershensky, where are we to keep this man until the submarine arrives?" He pointed a bony finger at the Death Merchant. "He is a very dangerous man and we have no facilities for prisoners. What are we to do with him?"

"He is my concern and responsibility, Dr. Borsilinskow," Vershensky said, his sharp tone matched only by his rapier-like stare. "I can assure you, he will not interfere with your work."

"Enough of this nonsense, Comrade General Vershensky," the scientist said. "I am not one of your agents. The Death Merchant is *our* responsibility, Comrade General Vershensky. Or have you forgotten that you and I share the command of this base? If you have, I shall be glad to have the Soviet Academy of Science remind you through the Presidium, if necessary. Again I ask you, where are we to keep this man? What security measures will be taken to protect us from him?"

"He shall be guarded day and night," Vershensky said, fighting hard to control his dignity. "There is no danger. Did he escape from the *Mikhail Lomonosov*, or from *Sovietskaya* I? Comrade Captain Yubishkanonavitch and his agents of the KGB did an excellent job. They will do just as good a job here at Zemlya II."

Colonel Pyotr Wrangel reinforced his boss' statement by saying, "Do not tell us how to do our job, Citizen Borsilinskow. While you share command with Comrade General Vershensky, security is strictly within the province of the KGB."

"Comrade General Vershensky, we can neutralize the Death Merchant with prolixin," suggested Captain Yubishkanonavitch. "As you know, sir, the drug is very effective!"

"We will not use prolixin." General Vershensky shook

his head. "We will not use any drugs. He must be fresh and mentally alert when he reaches Moscow. Those are the orders from the center."

"Where shall we put him?" Yubishkanonavitch asked.

"Secure his wrists and ankles with manacles, and take him to one of the store rooms in Dome III. I want two men with him day and night, four when he has his meals or goes to the toilet."

Vershensky finished lighting his cigarette, then looked at Dr. Lexi Borsilinskow. "Does that satisfy you, Citizen Borsilinskow?"

"If he escapes, the responsibility shall fall on your head," the scientist said simply. "This installation cost hundreds of millions of rubles and must be protected at all costs."

Camellion, still struggling to resume his calm, as if it were a coat and he couldn't find the sleeves, had been worried for a few moments. The drug Prolixin, called the "liquid straight jacket," was a tranquilizer fifty times more powerful and potent than Thorazine. It turned a man into a vegetable, induced a catatoniclike state and could cause a possible palsy syndrome. *One shot of Prolixin and I'd be finished!*

"General Vershensky, there is one thing I'd like for you to do," Camellion said. "It's a small thing, but I'm sure you'll comply."

Vershensky's eyes narrowed in curiosity. "Yes?"

"Could I have a pair of coveralls that fit?"

Chapter Five

The Death Merchant had to remind himself every now and then that he was still on earth and not on some watery world in another solar system. He certainly found it difficult to tell the difference when he looked at the transparent ceiling of the second floor room to which the KGB guards had taken him. Beyond the

66

ceiling, beyond the roof, was the "outside," the area surrounding the two-story cube. There were nine other cubes in Dome 3 and they were constructed of liquid concrete sprayed over steel mesh welded to I-beams. The Russians called the deep-blue-painted cubes "blue igloos."

All around the blue cubes, in a giant circle, was the concave dome, curving itself in and up over the flat roofs of the cubes until, at its highest point, it was thirty feet above the roof of the cube in which Camellion was a prisoner.

Beyond the dome on all sides, pressing against it with millions of pounds of pressure and billions of tons of water, was the Arctic Ocean. The sodium-vapor lights made the icy water glow with polychromatic color, almost as if the water were alive with some strange phosphorescent life all its own.

At times, glancing up in wonderment at the water fifty feet above his head, Camellion got the impression that the ocean was an unhallowed garden of grotesque efflorescence, a dark world of brooding evil just waiting . . . waiting for him . . . waiting to smother him, to fill his lungs with pressing, frigid death. Yet he knew there was life in those waters. He couldn't see it, but he knew it was there. And it was. There were jellyfish, trailing skeins of stinging tentacles. There were amphipods sprawled on the soft underbellies of the jellyfish, as if riding sun-tinted clouds. These tiny crustaceans, which flourished in Arctic waters, used the jellyfish as a mobile restaurant, sneaking scraps of food they caught or, at times, turning hungrily on their hosts themselves. There were little mollusks on the sea floor and ctenophores that glided along like three-inch-long, half-inflated footballs; and anchored to the ocean's floor were vivid holothurians, thrusting out branching tentacles in search of plankton.

Because the KGB agents were afraid of the Death Merchant, they had not taken that first chance with him. While he had still been before General Vershensky, Captain Yubishkanonavitch had carefully handcuffed his wrists behind his back before the five agents had marched him to the warehouse cube in Dome 3.

Now, several hours later, the five hog pen pilgrims were still with the Death Merchant, who sat on a folding chair in the center of the room which was filled with cardboard cartons and wooden crates of various sizes. It irked Camellion that one crate was marked *Peaches. Nimrod Food Stores. New York, New York.* By God, Lenin may have been right. The West just might hang itself with its own capitalist noose! Selling anything to the Communists was as silly as making an alcoholic the manager of a liquor store!

Escape was impossible, even for the Death Merchant. Two guards sat in front of Camellion, stun-guns held loose in their hands. Three agents were to Camellion's rear, Paruir Lovaya holding a cocked and ready-to-fire Stechkin machine pistol in his right hand.

The only thing that didn't worry Camellion was his ability to kill himself! He could even knock himself off here in the store room if he had to. He had already made a trial run. There was an enclosed toilet on the first floor of the blue igloo which Camellion had used. The goons had marched him to the first floor and had kept him covered with stun-guns and machine pistols while the slant-eyed Paruir Lovaya had unlocked his handcuffs. Camellion had then gone into the stall, Lovaya permitting him to close the door. Why not? How could he escape?

It would not have been a problem for Camellion to have removed the tiny strip of Napaprene pasted over the little fingernail of his left hand and to have put it in his mouth. Unconsciousness would have dropped over him in a few seconds, death following a few minutes later.

There was another particle of Napaprene he could have used, this one attached to the nail of his great toe on his right foot. Both strips had been impregnated with E-9z, a CIA-developed poison which was a combination of a substance that came from the sex organs of the Japanese globe-fish and a refined toxin made from cobra venom. As little as ten grams of E-9z could kill 10,000 people, if distributed properly. Combined, Camellion's two strips had .0001 percent of E9z, enough to kill him a hundred times over.

68

But not yet! Suicide was the last desperate measure, and the time was not yet. There was still hope—maybe.

At least, he mused, *I have a pair of coveralls that fit!*

He sat, his hands handcuffed behind his back, thinking gloomy thoughts, thinking that for a KGB general, Comrade Vershensky was one hell of a dumbbell. At the last moment, Vershensky had ordered Yubishkanona-vitch not to use manacles on Camellion's ankles.

"He knows there is no place he can run to," Vershen-sky had said. "And why shouldn't we permit him to exercise his legs now and then?"

He had turned to Camellion, his face very serious. "You see, Mr. Camellion, I am not a cruel man. We Russians always have compassion, even for an enemy of the state."

You're not a very clever man either! the Death Merchant had thought. *If you think your phony act is going to make me think about joining the KGB team, you're worse than crazy!*

An hour after Camellion had eaten a meal of sausage washed down with hot tea, someone knocked on the metal door of the second floor storage room. Instantly the guards were on full alert.

With Stechkin in hand, the chunky Paruir Lovaya walked quickly to the door, opened it, and stared at the middle-aged woman who wore a gray lab coat and carried a metal clipboard in her hand.

Lovaya pushed his bull-like head forward and looked at the photograph on the identification card pinned to the left lapel. Then he stared hard at the woman.

"What do you want?" he asked. "No one is allowed around the *Amerikanski* spy."

The heavyset woman made an angry face. "I didn't come here to see the bourgeois dog. But I must record the temperature and humidity."

"The temperature and humidity?" Lovaya echoed suspiciously.

"Temperature and humidity is recorded every three hours in each dome. Now let me in, Comrade, or should I report you to Comrade Dr. Lexi Borsilinskow and tell him that you are interfering with my work?

Remembering how General Vershensky had told Dr. Borsilinskow that the KGB would not interfere with the scientists, Lovaya did not argue with the woman, who looked at him as if he were a cockroach as he opened the door and she swept past him.

Lovaya closed the door, his eyes following her as she went across the room to the left-hand corner of the back wall. Attached to the wall was a two-foot-long thermometer of the Reaumur Fahrenheit variety. Next to the thermometer hung a Weiss hygrometer; between the two was a large card giving the readings of the errors of parallax in regard to recording the proper temperature.

Remaining by the door, Lovaya watched as the woman reached underneath her smock, took out a pen, and began to record the readings. After a few minutes she turned, walked to the center of the room, and stopped to return the pen to the inside pocket of her smock.

Comrade Lovaya waited impatiently. The two seated guards in front of Camellion also gave her the eye, while the three agents behind the Death Merchant ignored her out of necessity because their backs were to her.

Lovaya saw the woman's hand with the pen go underneath her lab coat, and he saw the same hand when it came out. In fact, her hand and the Makarov pistol with silencer attached was the very last thing he saw in this life. The automatic went *bbzzzzzzttttt*, and the last thing Lovaya felt in this life was a brief flash of agony as the 9mm slug entered his chest and burst his heart like an overinflated balloon. With an unbelievable look of disbelief, he sank to the floor, the Stechkin machine pistol slipping from his dead fingers.

Although he was as surprised as the guards, the Death Merchant, whose back was also to the woman, knew at once that she had put a slug into Lovaya. Ignoring the fact that his hands were handcuffed behind the chair, he threw himself and the chair sideways to the floor. A moment later the stunned guards recovered their senses, the two in front jumping to their feet and raising their stun-guns, the three to Camellion's rear reaching in desperation for their holstered machine pistols.

There were two more fast *bbzztts*, and slug-burned

holes appeared in the chests of the uniforms of the two men with stun-guns. They cried out, jerked, and died. The other three guards followed. One KGB boob, his pistol half-clearing its holster, took a slug in the chest. He snorted through his nose, closed his eyes, and went down. Another man got the big business an inch above his belt buckle. He dropped his Stechkin and sank to his knees. The third KGB agent received a scorching benediction several inches below the hollow of his throat. With waves of blood bubbling from his slack mouth, he crashed down, falling across the man who had been crossed out with a 9mm in his chest. The last sound "bloody mouth" heard was a faint *bbzztt* from the woman's Makarov as she put another bullet into the man who was moaning on the floor, his hands pressed over his stomach. The man stopped moaning. He stopped living, too.

Lying on his right side, Camellion tried to look up at the woman, who hurried toward him, then leaned down and whispered, *Saddlesoap: Two Bars!* I am Doctor Raya Dubanova, Mr. Camellion. Which one of them has the keys to your handcuffs?"

"Godzilla over there, the one dead by the door!" Camellion said.

"Who?" The scientist blinked at him in confusion, the name being decidedly not Russian.

"The slant-eyed corpse by the door," Camellion said. "Hurry! We don't have any time to spare."

The woman soon found the keys in the left coat pocket of the dead Paruir Lovaya, and soon Camellion's wrists were free. He got to his feet, rubbing his wrists, his eyes studying Raya Dubanova, who, weighing close to 200 pounds, was not a beauty. If she had not been wearing a lab coat, she would have looked a typical peasant woman (built like an ox and twice as strong) whom one sees on a collective farm. Her hair, combed straight back and knotted on the back of her head, didn't do anything for her either.

"You're taking a chance, Raya Dubanova," Camellion said. "Won't Vershensky and his boys know it was you who set me free—and where do we go from here?"

He leaned down, pulled two machine pistols from the

holsters of the dead guards, stood up, and stuffed them into the deep front pockets of his mechanics coveralls.

"The General won't suspect me," Dr. Dubanova replied. She pushed another clip into the handle of her pistol, cocked it by pulling back the slide, then thumbed on the safety catch. "I told the guards the truth. The temperature and humidity is taken every three hours, and it is part of my job to record the readings. I'm not only an engineer and meteorologist, I am also an environmentalist. How else could I have come to this blue igloo without raising suspicion?"

"But like I said, where do we go from here—and I mean we!" the Death Merchant said. "My job is to get you out of Zemlya II and I intend to do just that, or die trying!"

"Our only chance is to reach one of the "little-boats" in the lock-out chamber in Dome 1," Dr. Dubanova explained in a low, nervous voice, "the type of small submarine that brought you to Zemlya II. I can operate such a vehicle, but I do not know of any way we can reach the lock-out chamber. Another problem is that a "little-boat" has a range of only eighty miles. Unless the submarine that brought you from *Amerika* can pick us up, we will have no place to go. We will be stranded in the ocean."

She regarded him questioningly, waiting for him to commit himself.

The Death Merchant's icy blue eyes flickered in caution. Raya Dubanova had given the correct code-signal, but could he trust her completely? Why not? Anyhow— *do I have a choice?*

"You've overlooked a couple of more problems," Camellion said. "In order to contact the *Albacore*, I'll have to get the control center. I assume that's where communication is? I can use a code I know the KGB can't break. Even if they could, by the time they did it would be too late. We'll be in the *Albacore* and long gone, but only if we can escape in a "little-boat" to begin with!"

Raya Dubanova glanced nervously toward the door. "What is the second problem?"

"There's more than one of those little subs down in the

l.o.c.," Camellion said. "What's to prevent Vershensky and his boys from following us, although they couldn't do anything about it, except radio our position to any Russian full-sized sub that might be in the area. That would be bad enough. They could blow us out of the water!"

Raya Dubanova shook her head. "You are wrong. Some of the small submarines have lock-out chambers. Should we be followed, divers could board our vessel or plant charges against the hull of our craft. There is only one way we can insure our safety. We will have to blow up the l.o.c. in the control dome."

Amazed at the Russian woman's utter ruthlessness, the Death Merchant wondered why she was so willing to kill her own people. But her reasons were her business. Her father had died in one of Stalin's Gulags. A NSA agent had told Camellion in Washington. Could that be the reason?

"Wouldn't such an explosion destroy all of Zemlya II?" Camellion asked. "There's something else I'd like to know: what are the domes made of?"

Raya Dubanova hurriedly explained the facts of Zemlya II life to the Death Merchant. The first dome was the control center. It contained communications and fourteen special air pumps which not only supplied and regenerated air for breathing purposes but also kept up the fanatastic pressure in the five domes; this pressure, in combination with the strength of the domes, held back the Arctic Ocean. The domes were made of a substance which, once Raya Dubanova had named it, Camellion could only translate as "polychrome plastic." The new material had been invented by I.E.V. Kulinin, a Russian metallurgist.

"Tests show that it's harder than battleship armor," Raya Dubanova said. "We often call it 'transparent steel.'"

An explosion big enough to wreck the lock-out chamber in Dome 1 would not destroy the entire base, not even all of Dome 1. The polychrome wall, sealing off the l.o.c. from the rest of the control dome, was of sufficient strength to absorb the blast. There was further protection in that each dome there was a "blue igloo," which was actually a diving chamber with its own air supply. In case of an emergency, the people in each dome could ride out the storm in the square bathyspheres. Should the domes collapse, the Russians in the bathyspheres could float to the surface in the life-saving chambers.

"The greatest danger is the air pumps," Dr. Dubanova said. "If they should suddenly cease to operate, within twenty minutes the air pressure within the domes would drop to a point which would put the interior of the domes at a lower pressure than the ocean outside. If that happened, not even the strength of the 'transparent steel' could stop the ocean from collapsing all five domes."

Another problem! Where would the Death Merchant get the explosives to destroy the l.o.c. in Dome 1?

"Futhermore, I'll have to have the electronic components to make timers," Camellion said. "We have to have enough time to get out of the lock tube before the docks blow up!"

"I took care of that a week ago," Raya Dubanova said. "Over a period of months I took parts from our laboratory to make twenty-three battery-powered timers. I brought them with me, and have them hidden on the first floor." She looked at her wrist watch. "Holy God!" she exclaimed. "Time is fleeing from us. Come, we must hurry. I have a change of clothing for you that will help you get to Dome 2." She placed a hand on Camellion's arm. "Come, please. In another twenty minutes I must be in Dome 1."

Why Dome 2? Camellion assumed that the explosives were kept in Dome 2. He had assumed right. Raya Dubanova explained the layout of Zemlya II as she and Camellion crept down the narrow steel steps to the first floor of the blue igloo. Dome 1 was the control center—that he already knew. The dome in which they stood, number 3, was used only for storage. The laboratories were in Dome 4, while Dome 5 was used to quarter the scientists and technicians.

Which left Dome 2. "General Vershensky and his staff, as well as the regular KGB agents, live in Dome 2," Raya Dubanova said hesitantly, almost as if she were afraid that if she told the truth, Camellion might lose his nerve. "One of the igloos in the armory. The first floor contains arms and ammunition. The explosives are on the second floor."

A worried look crossed Camellion's tanned face. "What kind of explosives. I have to know what I'm working with!"

"The Russian name is of no importance," Raya Dubanova said, looking cautiously around the first floor room in which only a small twenty-watt bulb burned. "But it's nitrostarch. They come packed in one and five pound blocks. The geologists use the explosive for blasting on the sea bottom." She inhaled loudly, her ample bosom rising and falling rapidly with excitement. "The igloo which houses the explosives is painted red, and I must tell you that it is well guarded. Even down here, five hundred feet below the surface of the ocean, the KGB trusts no one. Wait!"

Dr. Dubanova hurried to a small round window and carefully looked beyond the room, her sharp gaze sweeping the unnatural man-made landscape, the steel lawn and the blue igloos clustered around like gigantic metal and concrete boils. Beyond them was the dome of "transparent steel"—and the Arctic Ocean.

The Death Merchant finished stuffing his shirt into his pants, then buckled the belt of the pants. Nitrostarch! *Oh boy!* Of all the high explosives in the world, nitrostarch was one of trickiest, far more sensitive to flame, friction, and impact than either TNT or tetrytol. *Fudge, you can't break or crush the blocks without risking their blowing up! Some mess I've gotten myself into—all for a lousy five hundred grand.*

On the other hand, he concluded, half a million tax-free American dollars would help a lot of poor people in Texas and put quite a few deserving youngsters through college. *Yeah, the risk is worth it!*

Frustration churning within him, he watched Dr. Raya Dubanova turn from the small oval window and go to one side of the room. She reached around a crate close to the wall and pulled out a bundle of clothing and a small fiberboard suitcase. Then she hurried back to Camellion, put the suitcase on the floor, and handed him the bundle of clothing tied together with a cord.

"Put these on, Death Merchant" she ordered, and waddled back to the window, moving surprisingly fast for a woman of her bulk.

With one quick motion, Camellion broke the cord, and laid out the lab clothes across a box. Wondering if the rubber stockings were the kind that were normally worn or if they were some kind of equipment, Camellion started to change clothes.

"Doctor, I want some information about the tubes connecting the domes," he said, slipping into the gray lab pants. "When the guards brought me here, I noticed a bulkhead at each end of the tube. There weren't any guards stationed in the tubes; yet the doors opened at our approach. Are the doors operated by photoelectric cells?"

"That is correct. The doors are operated on the command electronic lock principle," Raya Dubanova replied without turning from the window. "I must warn you about those doors; they can be a false security to what you must do. The double doors at each end of each tube can be automatically locked from the control center in Dome 1. It is imperative that you, that we, reach the lock-out chamber in Dome 1 before Security discovers that you have escaped."

The Death Merchant, annoyed at the woman's assumption that he could accomplish the impossible, finished buttoning the shirt. "I suppose you realize I'll have to make myself invisible to get the job done. I'll be lucky if I can even get to the explosives in Dome 2!"

He put on the lab coat, picked up the two loaded Stechkins, jammed them in his belt, then picked up the half dozen spare clips and dropped them into a pocket of the coat.

"With the help of God, you will succeed, Mr. Camellion!" Raya Dubonova said fiercely. She turned from the window and stared at him, her eyes flaming with messianic passion. "I will pray that we will succeed, and with His help we will. Have faith in the Lord, Mr. Camellion. God will protect you!"

The Death Merchant, whose acute sense of intuition

never failed him, stabbed Raya Dubanova with a look of sheer pity, a ding-dong alarm gonging in his brain. Raya Dubanova was a religious nut!

By the blue beard of Baal! A Commie Christian crackpot!

Her very manner, the fanatical look in her eyes, was proof that her whole being was submerged in a cesspool of superstition. The Death Merchant knew from experience that it would have been a sheer waste of time to tell her that even though God might be alive and well and well-meaning, he was hopelessly inefficient. And so the machinery of life had to stagger on murderously by itself.

God? Down here at the bottom of the Arctic Ocean? Down here in this world of steel and polychrome steel? *Uh huh . . . and the Word was made steel . . . born of the Immaculate Manufacture!* Ah, but not on the surface world where Billy Graham and other television entertainers spread a lot of fear but damned little morality. But what else could the hell-shouting evangelists do but pander to public taste? Homo sapiens in all his superstitious glory demanded a jealous and sadistic god.

Camellion picked up the suitcase of timers, walked over to Dr. Raya Dubanova, and looked out the oval window. Parked in front of the blue igloo were two sub-shuttle cars, the one Dr. Dubanova was using and the one the KGB had used to transport Camellion from the control dome to Dome 3. The area was clear of Russians, since this was a storage dome without workers.

"Doctor, you go first," Camellion said. "I'll wait five minutes and follow. That should give you time to get through Dome 2 and reach the control dome. But how long will you be there? Where can I find you?"

Dr. Dubanova looked at her wrist watch. "I go off duty in an hour and twenty-two minutes. By then, if not before, the KGB will have discovered that you have escaped. This means that I will be in Comrade General Vershensky's office being questioned, since taking the readings in this dome is a part of my duties. But the KGB will not suspect me. I am a trusted and exceptional worker. How you will get to me in Comrade Vershensky's office"—she made a helpless gesture with her hands—"is a problem you must solve."

"With God's help, I suppose!" Richard said resentfully, feeling frustration almost overpower him. He was faced with the impossible!

His derogatory remark brought a quick but quiet condemnation from the Russian scientist, who said in a low, soft voice, "Mr. Camellion, it is a mistake to condemn a belief because you yourself have doubts. In the West, the present Christian tendency to suspect divine power as immoral and to emphasize Christ as the principle of love is partly a consequence of the decline of belief and is partly responsible for it. Men require a god they can fear. And still people want to be loved and supported by the divine, because they are helpless and afraid and need the love of a god who is strong, just as children find strength in their parents, as well as love and mercy."

"You should add that if a god must be all-powerful, he must be dangerous," Camellion said lazily, putting his hand on the doorknob. "However, this is not the time and place for a lecture on religion. Before we go, suppose you tell—"

"I am aware that like Marx you equate religious belief with weakness," Dr. Dubanova went on, as if she hadn't heard him. "If religion is a crutch, it is a very necessary and stabilizing one."

"Millions of people say the same thing about alcohol, tobacco, and drugs," Camellion cut in viciously. "As far as I'm concerned, religion is the worst moral evil on the face of the earth, next to Communism. It's an evolution toward debasement, with the survival of the unfittest! Personally, I don't give a damn if you want to worship the moon, but I don't like to think of myself as being the victim of either a sardonic joker or a whimsical tyrant; and I despise any system that forbids man to think and to reason. That's what your damned Christianity does, in all its forms: it makes man a moral slave and would deny him his right to reason! Now, suppose we stop discussion on morality and you tell me the ultra-secret information you're supposed to have, just in case I am able to escape and you don't make it."

Alarm and fear flashed over the pale fat face of Raya Dubanova, an acute apprehension that baffled the Death Merchant, who watched the mysterious dread rise and swim unchecked in her dark eyes.

"No!" she gasped hoarsely, her breathing labored. "Not here, Mr. Camellion. The information is too horrible to discuss here, too unbelievable. Yes, perhaps even too dangerous. If I told you the secret and you were captured and made to talk." She shook her head emphatically. "I won't tell you until we are safe! Why I don't even know if I can trust the high officials in your own government!"

Richard Camellion didn't like paradoxes. "Then why did you agree to work for the CIA?" he asked, his voice sharp with impatience.

"I didn't agree to work for your *Amerikanski* spy organization!" replied Raya Dubanova bitterly, her shock quickly dying in the realization that the Death Merchant was laboring under a misconception. "I would never consider being a traitor to Mother Russia any more than I could ever respect the lies and hypocrisy of your own government in *Amerika*. We in the Soviet Union are aware of how your president favors big business, especially the large oil interests, while at the same time taking free lunches and food stamps from the mouths of school children and poor people. We know this is not propaganda. Not all that Pravda prints is a lie!"

"Then what was your purpose in contacting the CIA?"

"Because we—I and five other scientists—realized that our own Communist government would not believe us!" Raya Dubanova whispered, spreading her hands in a gesture of helplessness. "The Kremlin will not consider any theory that does not fit into the framework of Marxism. I ask you, what other large government on this earth is left, other than your United States?"

"All right, Doctor," Camellion said calmly, his manner iceberg efficient. Gently, he opened the door and motioned to it with one of the Stechkin machine pistols he had pulled from his belt. "I'll grab you out of Comrade Vershensky's office—God willin' and if the creek don't rise! God be with you, Raya Dubanova!"

Not knowing whether the Death Merchant was sincerely wishing her well or if his last phrase was meant as a final mocking insult, Dr. Dubanova hurried through the door. She didn't look back. She walked to the sub-shuttle electric car, climbed into the front seat, and started the battery-powered engine—still unable to explain to herself what the rise of a creek had to do with either success or failure! Who could understand *Amerikanskis!* A people who laughed a lot, yes! But still odd.

She turned the humming six-wheeled car around and headed for the bulkhead in the end of the tube connecting Dome 3 with Dome 2. The Death Merchant watched from the window, staring after the car as it approached the bulkhead, which was sixty feet in front of him and two hundred feet to his right. When the car was thirty feet from the round steel lock, the rounded double doors parted in the center and silently swung inward against the sides of the polychrome plastic tube, permitting the sub-shuttle car to enter. The car entered the lock and the double doors immediately closed.

Why wait five minutes? From his position in the blue igloo, Richard couldn't see the other end of the tube, the end that opened into Dome 2. He didn't have to see the other end. The length of the connecting tube was only fifty feet. By now, Doctor Dubanova had to be zipping through Dome 2 on her way to the control center in the first dome

OK, let's have a go at it! I've got nothing to lose but my life. Camellion thrust the machine pistol back into his waist and buttoned the lab coat, leaving it open close to the butts of both Stechkins. Walking at a normal pace, he left the square concrete-and-steel building, strode to the other sub-shuttle car, settled himself behind the wheel and pressed the green starter button.

He was halfway to the lock in the tube when the lock on the other side of the dome swung open and a sub-shuttle car came through the opening from Dome 4. Expecting trouble, the Death Merchant slowed his own vehicle while the car zipped by, the four men in the odd-looking car—three dressed in lab clothes, the fourth man in the blue uniform of a KGB security agent—not even glancing in his direction.

When their car reached the proper distance from the end of the lock in the tube connecting Dome 3 with Dome 2, the lock in Dome 3 swung open and the car shot through the circular opening. This time, however, the double doors of the lock only half closed, the front tires of Camellion's vehicle, thirty feet in front of the lock, going over that section of metal flooring that triggered the photoelectric cell-controlled opening mechanism. The semicircular doors swung back, and Camellion's car entered the tube, Camellion refusing to look at the roof of the tube no more than fifteen feet above his head, at the faintly chemicoluminescent water on the other side of the polychrome plastic tube—above him, and to his left and to his right. It was as though he were travelling through a tunnel in the Arctic Ocean, but a tunnel with nothing holding the water back! *Now I know how Moses and his guys felt when they ran through the waters of the Red Sea!*

It was only a few seconds after Camellion had entered the tube that the lock doors at the opposite end swung open as his car triggered the photo-electric device. Its engine humming like a swarm of sleepy bees, the sub-shuttle car zipped through the lock into Dome 2, the Death Merchant slowing the machine as the lock closed behind him and the car that had passed him in Dome 3 breezed through the tube that led to Dome 1.

Here I am! Now how to do it! Slowing the car even more, the Death Merchant analyzed the set-up in Dome 2, each small detail burning into his mind. Almost in the center of the dome was the two-story igloo containing the arms, ammo, and explosives, its exterior painted as red as the royal roses Camellion's mother used to grow in St. Louis, Missouri, USA.

In front of the armory, lounging on folding chairs, were three uniformed KGB security agents, their AK-47 assault rifles leaning against the side of the building. One of the pig farmers was reading a book (probably Marx); the other two Slavic hay rakers were laughing and talking.

At one front corner of the armory was a tall metal pole, to the tip of which was attached a grim-looking siren. Overhead, hanging from the ceiling of the dome, were the four round sodium-vapor lights, splashing a bluish white glow over the entire area.

Other than the armory, there were eight other igloos in the dome, three to the left of the barn-red building, three to the right, one in front, and one behind, the igloo in front having a rounded roof studded with rivet heads; at the top, in the center of the rounded roof-dome, was a hatch. Camellion knew that igloo was the emergency escape diving chamber.

To make him feel even more like a damn fool determined to commit suicide, there were seven KGB hot-shots in goggles and shorts, sunbathing to the right of the first igloo left of the armory. Attached to a wire, strung from a front corner of the armory to a back corner of the first igloo, were half a dozen heat lamps, their ultraviolet quartz tanning tubes and infrared heat rods flooding the men, lying on rubber mats.

In the space between the armory and the middle igloo, which was to the right of the armory, three men, in gray sweatsuits, were exercising on rings and parallel bars.

Besides the guards in front of the armory, Camellion spotted another danger. To the left of the igloo that was the diving chamber, three workers, under the watchful eyes of three KGB guards, were unloading bottles of oxygen mixture from a flat-bedded, rubber-tired wagon attached to a tractorlike vehicle which resembled a sub-shuttle car, except that it was twice as large and had a small canopy over the driver's compartment in the rear. Camellion surmised that the workers were taking recharged tanks into the igloo escape chamber.

Another question: how many more KGB men were in the igloos?

During those five seconds, while the car had travelled halfway the distance to the lock of the tube leading to Dome 1, Camellion had made up his mind what to do. He pulled a machine pistol from underneath his lab coat, turned the car sharply to the right, and increased speed.

The siren on top of the metal pole began to shriek. *I-ouega-I-ouega-I-ouega.* His escape had been discovered!

The Death Merchant, feeling as if he had been hit

in the face with a sock filled with ice cubes, remembered Raya Dubanova's warning about the locks:

"The double doors at the end of each tube can be automatically locked from the control center in Dome 1!" she had said.

Trapped!

Chapter Six

Used only for the most dangerous of emergencies, the screaming siren did wonders for the KGB personnel in Dome 2. Thinking that the day of doom was about to befall the domes of Zemlya II, the sun-bathers jumped up, jerked off their goggles, and stared around them like man trapped naked in the middle of Main Street. The men unloading the oxygen bottles and the KGB agents with them reacted in a similar manner, freezing up for a split second and looking up in fear at the curved top of the vast polychrome plastic dome. So did the three KGB guards in front of the armory. Collectively then, the men saw the sub-shuttle car racing toward the blue igloos, its driver hunched as low as he could in the front seat; then they remembered the Death Merchant.

The Russians were positive the alarm was screaming the escape of the Death Merchant when his car came straight at the escape-to-the-surface-chamber igloo and Camellion opened fire on the KGB guards, who were only moments away from levelling down on him with their Ak-47 assault rifles.

The machine pistol in Camellion's right hand roared, and while the three workers dove for cover, two of the guards went down with 9mm slugs in their chests. The third pig farmer was about to open fire when he caught a 9mm piece of steel in the shoulder, the impact half-spinning him around and causing reflex to make him jerk up the barrel of the AK and his finger to tighten on the trigger. The automatic rifle snarled, the stream of 7.62mm slugs striking the curved ceiling of the dome and ricocheting off the steel-hard plastic.

Unarmed, the half-nude sun-bathers made a dash-for-life to the rear of the second igloo to the left of the armory.

With its throttle wide open, the sub-shuttle car hummed toward the front of the armory at forty-six m.p.h., its square green front centered on the double doors of the red building. Although the doors were made of aluminum sheeting, they were hollow and only several inches thick—so Camellion assumed, comparing them to the door of the storage igloo in which he had been held prisoner.

The KGB guards weren't fools. When they saw the car coming straight at them and the maniac driving it, they fired off short bursts from their AKs, then jumped to one side to prevent the car from crushing them to a pulp.

The AK slugs didn't shatter the windshield because there was no windshield. They didn't shatter the Death Merchant because there was no Death Merchant. Camellion had ducked down low in the front seat, and even though a couple of dozen 7.62mm slugs had chopped through the grill-like front of the car, the metal interior had prevented them from reaching him. The slugs did short-circuit the electric car, slowing it down, but not enough to prevent its momentum from carrying it forward toward the double doors of the armory.

The car crashed into the double doors, ripping the aluminum with a loud tearing sound. The impact stopped the car; yet the force carried half of it through the double doors and ripped them from their hinges. They hung at a crooked angle, supported only by the car thrust into their middle like some unwanted obscene intruder.

His ears still ringing from the crash, the Death Merchant practically fell out of the front seat onto the metal floor of the armory, a floor that was covered with wooden slats.

There were no windows in the building, and the car was wedged in the building so tightly that Camellion had to look outside by going to one end of the double doors, to where they had been pulled from the hinges in the wall and there was a three-foot gap.

Both Stechkin machine pistols in his hands, the Death Merchant couldn't see a single pig farmer. Then he spotted the muzzles of several AKs poking from around the front corner of the igloo to his left. Just as the Russians opened fire, he dropped flat and rolled to the front of the sub-shuttle car. Seven more KGB boys joined in—two from the corner of the igloo in front and to the right of the armory, and three from the front right-hand corner of the escape-to-the-surface igloo. The hot steel from the nine automatic rifles filled the space between the door and the wall with a tidal wave of pure 7.62mm death. With loud high-pitched zings, the slugs ricocheted off the wrecked car and the stacked boxes of arms and ammunition behind the Death Merchant.

As suddenly as the firing had started, it stopped. The Death Merchant heard an angry voice shout frantically from the front of the igloo to his left: "Don't fire you idiots! If a bullet hits a hand grenade and it explodes, everything will explode, and the entire dome will go up!"

Camellion grinned crookedly, then wondered why he was smiling. It might be a Mexican standoff—*but I'm the one who's bottled up!* Hand grenades? He looked around him, reading the stenciled lettering on the boxes and crates neatly stacked, almost to the ceiling, on three sides of the room.

The bottom section of the armory was indeed an arsenal. There were crates of Tokarev and Makarov pistols, and box after box of Stechkin machine pistols, as well as long cartons filled with AK-47 assault rifles, Dragunov submachine guns, and SKS carbines. A dozen boxes whose markings indicated they contained the new 9mm sixteen-shot Vitmorkin machine pistol that Camellion had heard so much about. Cases of ammunition for all the various kinds of weapons, along with boxes of hand grenades, ammo belts, grenade bags, and other equipment. More than a dozen crates were packed with ShKAS light machine guns.

Camellion stared at half a dozen of the stacked cases. *They've even got RPG-7 rocket launchers and rockets to match! Why?* Richard asked himself. Why this arsenal—enough to equip a battalion—at the bottom of the ocean? There was only one logical answer: Zemlya II was a storage depot, a dispersal center for arms the Russians furnished to various revolutionary groups around the world. It was easy for Richard to imagine these weapons being landed at night, from a submarine, on some lonely coast. From this point at the top of the world, a Soviet U-boat could go south to almost any coastal nation on earth.

Another thing: all the crates were wood! Camellion stared at a box of hand grenades between two boxes of Vitmorkin machine pistols. The hand grenades, five feet off the floor, were in line with the space between one end of the wrecked doors and the end of the front wall. And there were three bullet holes in the side of the wooden crate. Why then hadn't the grenades exploded?

Camellion was about to crawl over to the grenades when a voice called out to him from the front of the escape-to-the-surface igloo—and in perfect English!

"Death Merchant! This is Captain Yegenni Molody. I call upon you to throw down your arms and surrender. Escape for you is impossible. Come out with your hands up. We promise humane treatment!"

Stalling for time, Camellion shouted back, "Give me five minutes to think it over. Stay back or I'll blow up this arsenal. If it goes, so will the entire dome."

Captain Molody called in return, "Five minutes. No more."

The Death Merchant didn't underestimate his position. Since there were no windows in the arsenal, the KGB boys would come up from behind the building, slip along the side of the front wall, and rush him by charging through the gaps between the ends of the front walls and the ends of the doors. Or some pig farmer might try to be a hero by crawling underneath the sub-shuttle car wedged in the wrecked doors. Due to the height of the six tires, there was ample room between the bottom of the car and the floor.

Camellion hurried across the room to a wrecking bar lying on a box. With the bar in one hand, and the Stechkin in the other, he ran to the box of hand grenades, jerked it to the floor, and tore off the top boards. He soon saw why the bullets had not detonated the grenades. The grenades were packed in some kind of bulletproof material—between the outside wood and the grenades was a sheet of transparent material about a quarter of an inch thick, as clear and as hard as glass. Polychrome plastic? No matter the composition of the material, it could stop long-range slugs. The bullets fired into the box were flattened out between the wood and the transparent material.

I've got to work fast! While keeping a wary eye on the two front gaps and the space underneath the sub-shuttle car, he took the wrecking bar and opened a crate filled with Vitmorkin machine pistols, receiving a pleasant surprise when he found that the weapons weren't packed in cosmoline. Well, well, each pistol was in an open leather holster on a belt to which was attached an ammo pouch filled with nine spare clips, each clip containing sixteen 9mm cartridges.

Richard pulled out two belts, removed the pistol in its holster and the ammo pouch from the first belt, and fastened them to the second one, which he buckled around his waist after discarding his lab coat.

He took the wrecking bar and in quick succession ripped open three more crates. Soon he had a fully loaded Dragunov submachine gun in his hands and two canvas holder bags on each hip, their thick straps criss-crossing his back and chest. One bag was filled with twelve Dragunov magazines, each magazine containing fifty 7.62mm cartridges. The second bag was empty. Camellion was filling it with hand grenades when he heard Captain Molody's voice for the second time.

"Death Merchant! It has been five minutes! Are you going to surrender?"

Camellion, puzzled over something that had been bothering him, called back, "Captain Molody, are you related to Konon Molody, the master spy who infiltrated British M16 under the name of 'Gordon Lonsdale?'"

"I'm his brother," Yegenni Molody replied. Then, in a very angry voice—"Do you surrender? This is your last chance!"

The Death Merchant smiled. "Not today! Not ever! Come and get me, pig farmer!"

Carrying the wrecking bar and the submachine gun, he ran across the room and slowly and carefully went up the steel steps to the second floor level, putting three 9mm slugs on five of the steps. Moments later he was in the upstairs, staring at the boxes neatly stacked from floor to almost the ceiling. On the side of each box was the word Raya Dubanova had used to indicate nitrostarch. Below the word, also printed in red, were the Russian words for "Danger" and "High Explosive."

The Death Merchant didn't have any doubts: this was the nitrostarch, packed in twenty-five pound and fifty pound wooden crates, a twisted rope handle attached to the ends of each crate.

All the while listening for any unusual noise from the metal steps, Camellion opened one of the fifty-pound crates. Unlike the boxes of arms and ammunition downstairs, these crates had hinged lids and were free of nails, as a safe-guard against static electricity.

Camellion pulled open the hasp and threw back the one-piece wooden lid. There it was, the nitrostarch, fifty one-pound blocks wrapped in slick brown paper. On each side of the box was an inch of cottonlike padding, and Camellion assumed there was more padding in the bottom of the box. He noticed, too, that between the padding and the wood of the box was a quarter of an inch of the hard, transparent material. Even the one-piece lid had a layer of the cottonlike padding, as well as the plastic material between wood and fluff.

Fudge! Camellion looked around the room. Box after box in row after row. There had to be 5,000 pounds of nitrostarch in this room, more than 4,800 times the amount needed to blow Dome 2 all over the bottom of the Arctic Ocean.

The Death Merchant had problems. He hadn't told Raya Dubanova, but destroying the lock-out chamber in the control dome was not possible. He wouldn't have the time to plant the charges in the proper places. There was a way, although it was one that out of necessity would destroy all of Zemlya II. Destroy the air compressors! Blow them up! Without air pressure, the domes could not hold back the ocean's water! Zemlya II would cease to exist.

But first—*I have to escape from here and get to the control dome! And how do I lug twenty-five pounds of nitrostarch around with me?*

Suddenly Camellion remembered. He had forgotten the bag of timers! He had left the small suitcase in the front seat of the wrecked sub-shuttle car! Suppose the KGB slobs found them?

To add to his troubles, he heard cartridges rolling on the metal steps!

Chapter Seven

Black and reddish purple, Raya Dubanova's right eye was swollen shut. Both sides of her face were bruised and three times their normal size, and her entire head throbbed with pain. Slumped in a chair in front of Comrade General Rostislav Vershensky's desk and barely conscious, she tasted not only blood from her cut mouth, but the bitterness of defeat, her despair made worse by her realization that it was her fault that Control had discovered the Death Merchant had escaped.

Now, Raya Dubanova regretted that after she had shot the KGB agents guarding Camellion in the storage igloo in Dome 3, she had not taken the precaution to put a bullet into the head of each man. If she had, one of the agents would not have been able to crawl to the telephone to mumble a dying warning to Control—a warning that Camellion had escaped, and that she, Raya Dubanova, had helped him do it by shooting the guards.

She had been taking readings in the vicinity of the air compressors when the siren had gone off. Moments later, the KGB had taken her into custody and had dragged her to its headquarters' dome, to Comrade General Vershensky's office. In a rage, Vershensky had questioned her, her denials of any wrongdoing bringing only a savage beating from Major Ivan Sedin while General Vershensky, Colonel Pyotr Wrangel, and Captain Vasily Tur called her a traitor and a murderer and urged her to confess. Why had she done it? Why had she helped the Death Merchant escape? What was the connection between her and the Death Merchant?

"Are you working for the Central Intelligence Agency?" they screamed at her!

Confess! Confess! Confess!

Finally, Dr. Dubanova had fainted. She came to minutes later, hearing Comrade General Vershensky speaking into the telephone. Through a fog of pain, she deduced from listening to his angry words that the Death Merchant had killed three KGB agents in Dome 2, was trapped in the armory, and had threatened to blow up the place. She hoped he would.

General Vershensky continued to listen on the phone, his heavily lidded eyes burning with hate and fury.

Raya Dubanova heard him growl into the phone, "Almost fifteen minutes? Then send your men in after him, Captain Molody. I want him alive, and don't you dare forget it!"

He paused, listening. Then he said, "Don't be a fool, Comrade Molody. He wouldn't dare blow up the dome. He is not the type to commit suicide!" Another brief pause. "Yes. I know you do not have tear gas. Send your men in with small arms only. The crates are protected. Small arms fire can't penetrate the polychrome plastic." Another pause. "I don't care if you do lose men. I want him taken alive—and that's a direct order! That's right. Call me the instant you have him in custody, and you'd better get him damned fast!"

General Vershensky banged down the phone on its cradle and stared at Dr. Dubanova. He sat on the front corner of his desk, one foot on the floor, the other foot swinging back and forth. Slowly he got up, went over to Raya Dubanova, grabbed her by the hair, and jerked her head back so that she was forced to look at him with her one good eye.

"Now, you traitorous bitch," he hissed, leaning down, "I want to know why you helped Camellion escape. Tell me, damn you!"

A great and desperate courage, born of a deep and fanatical hatred of Stalinism, welled up within Raya Dubanova. No longer did she care what they might do to her. Let the godless monsters pull her limb from limb! Let the KGB kill her. They would anyhow—eventually. No, she told herself. She would never give General Vershensky and his group of sadists the satisfaction of a single sensible answer.

She opened her mouth, the movement sending needles of pain throughout her face. "Comrade General Vershensky," she mumbled, "I will tell you this—go straight to hell!"

Vershensky hit the woman so hard with his open hand that the sound could be heard in an upstairs room where a KGB agent was filing the daily surveillance reports on the scientists and technicians who worked in Zemlya II. The blow made Raya Dubanova's brain shudder, and filled her ears with a great roaring agony. The large room began to swim around her; then the darkness closed in and she passed out once more.

Major Sedin stepped closer to the unconscious woman and pulled a pair of needle-nosed pliers from the left pocket of his uniform coat. A hard-faced man with a large mole on his chin, the major glanced at General Vershensky. "I'll make the bitch talk, Comrade General." he offered. "I'll revive her and pull out her fingernails, one by one, very slowly. If that doesn't do the trick, I'll start on her toes!"

"Why not burn her with cigarettes?" suggested Captain Vasily Tur. "I'm told that fire is the most agonizing kind of pain!"

Vershensky made a disapproving face, his expression one of utter disgust.

"No," he growled. "She is already marked too much. How can she go to trial without fingernails? All of you know how the center dislikes physical evidence of an interrogation. Well. they'll get the truth out of her when she reaches Moscow."

"It's too bad we don't have truth drugs here," Captain Vasily Tur said, patting the back of his blond wavy hair. He hesitated for a moment. "Perhaps if we dosed her with the punishment drug Anectine, she'd decide to tell

91

the truth. I am told Anectine makes one feel that he's paralyzed and drowning at the same time, that it's worse than dying."

"Don't be foolish," Colonel Wrangel snapped, frowning in disapproval. "Have you forgotten her medical record? We checked that before we went to work on the bitch. She's a diabetic. A shot of Anectine could kill her. Think of what the center would have to say about that! When Moscow hears what's happened, we'll have more than enough explaining to do. We—"

Wrangel, remembering that General Vershensky was present, suddenly stopped talking, thinking he had said enough, perhaps too much. Expecting a reprimand for speaking disrespectfully about the center, he avoided looking at Vershensky, who went around his desk, sat down in the swivel chair, and stared at the phone, hoping it would ring and bring news of the Death Merchant's capture.

Captain Tur glanced briefly at the unconscious Raya Dubanova and walked to the round window behind the general's desk. All was normal within the control dome. The only sign of an emergency was the platoon of guards stationed around the fourteen large air compressors and the guards under the command of Comrade Paul Yubishkanonavitch, thirty feet from the lock of the tube that opened into Dome 1. Using sub-shuttle cars, they had made a semicircular barricade and were crouched behind the vehicles, their Dragunovs, AK-47s, and SKS carbines aimed at the closed lock. There was even a heavy weapon, a ZPU-2 14.5mm heavy machine gun mounted on a sub-shuttle car, its twin barrels pointed at the closed lock. A flea couldn't have flown through the lock without getting splattered!

Major Ivan Sedin might have been monitoring Vasily Tur's thoughts, for he walked closer to General Vershensky's desk and said to the brooding KGB official, "Comrade General Vershensky, if we would send Comrade Yubishkanonavitch's platoon into Dome 2, they could facilitate the capture of the Death Merchant. We could open the locks only long enough for the platoon to get inside Dome 2. That way the Death Merchant could be captured more quickly."

"Comrade Major Sedin, you are not thinking logically," Vershensky said, looking up at Sedin, his voice irritated. "The air compressors and the communications igloo are the most important parts of Zemlya II. They must be protected at all costs. Comrade Yubishkanonavitch and his men will stay where they are."

"Don't talk foolishly, Comrade," Colonel Wrangel admonished Sedin, who always agreed with anything Vershensky said. If Vershensky had said that Jesus Christ was a two-headed Eskimo, Wrangel would have nodded and said, "that is right."

"To open the locks for only a few minutes would be to risk Camellion's reaching this dome," Wrangel went on. "He has to get to the lock-out chamber to escape. That's what he's trying to do, meet Raya Dubanova, get to the lock-out chamber, and escape in "little-boat." The damned swine!" He turned and spit with his eyes at Raya Dubanova who was unconscious, her head sagged to one side. "She is even worse; she's a traitor." His eyes went back to an uncomfortable Major Sedin, who had sat down close to the door. "What you have forgotten, Comrade, is that there are thirty-six off-duty men in Dome 2, more than enough to take care of the Death Merchant. Comrade Yubishkanonavitch and his men are not needed in there."

With a smug expression on his face, Colonel Wrangel went over to a small table on which a kettle of water was boiling and began to fix himself a cup of tea.

Captain Vasily Tur pulled up a chair and sat down in front of Vershensky's desk. "We're lucky the sub arrived ahead of schedule," he said carefully. "If the Death Merchant intended to escape with Comrade Dubanova in "little-boat," there has to be an American submarine somewhere not too far away. If there is, the *Sergeyevich Pushkin* will find her. The *Pushkin* is of the Delta class and can outmatch anything the Americans have."

"That's true," agreed Major Sedin, lighting a cigarette. "But it will almost be another two hours before the *Pushkin* is ready to go out on the hunt. By then, the Death Merchant will be our prisoner again. The *Pushkin* can take him and Dubanova both to Leningrad! What a coup that shall be for us!"

No one replied. General Vershensky continued to stare at the telephone on his desk, his eyes frozen, the thick fingers of his left hand tapping methodically on the glass-top. Colonel Wrangel, his back to the others, slowly stirred his cup of tea.

Vasily Tur did not dare say what he was really thinking; he was much too clever to make such a mistake. So, the comrade general had told Ivan that he was not thinking "logically." But it was Vershensky who was thinking illogically, just as it was Comrade Wrangel who was actually the fool. If the thirty-six men off duty in Dome 2 could take care of the Death Merchant, why was Comrade Yubishkanonavitch's platoon guarding the lock that opened into the control dome? There could be only one logical answer: because Comrade General Vershensky was afraid that the agents in Dome 2 could not capture the Death Merchant. The son of a bitch was putting on a big front, but he had a lot of doubts!

Captain Tur had always been fascinated by the study of logic, reading all he could find on Plato, Aristotle, and other ancient and modern logicians. In his own mind, he was positive that Vershensky—and Wrangel, too—were using *post hoc, ergo propter hoc* ("after this, therefore because of this") fallacies to rationalize why the Death Merchant had to be captured and why he would not blow up the dome! As Captain Tur saw the situation, there was no way to deduce what an incredible man like the Death Merchant might do, and Tur suspected that both Comrade Vershensky and Comrade Wrangel knew it, but couldn't bring themselves to admit it, not even to themselves.

Captain Tur turned and looked in feigned respect at General Vershensky, who leaned forward like a huge uniformed toad, banged his fist down on the desk top, and hissed, "I'm positive! The Death Merchant came to Zemlya II to effect the escape of Raya Dubanova. But why is she so important that the Death Merchant himself would come after her?"

Major Sedin became very attentive. Colonel Wrangel, a cup of tea in his hand, turned and faced the desk, his manner alert.

"Sir, there isn't any evidence that Comrade Doctor

Dubanova is in league with any of the other scientists," Major Sedin offered. "There's nothing suspicious about even her own loyalty file. Yet it is obvious that she has vital data which the Central Intelligence Agency wants—who else could he be working for?"

"The information has to be data about Zemlya II, what else?" Captain Tur said. "The center will get the full truth out of the bitch." He glanced at Raya Dubanova, who still sagged in the chair like a sack of dust. The only reason she hadn't toppled to the floor was that there was a strap around her chest holding her to the chair.

"She's still unconscious, but she seems to be coming around," Tur said.

"We'll take her to the infirmary as soon as the Death Merchant is captured," General Vershensky said, "and we'll have a serious talk with Dr. Borsilinskow and try to get to the bottom of this mess." When he saw the surprised looks on the faces of Tur and Sedin and Wrangel, he added emphatically, sounding as if he were making a pronouncement, "It won't make a damn bit of difference this time. The gravity of the situation won't permit him to say we're interfering with the work of his precious scientists, especially since it was one of his people who murdered three of ours. We have Borsilinskow, that bastard, where we want him, and there isn't anything he can do about it, no one he can complain to. Oh, sure, we'll question him and his people with respect, but we're not going to let one of them off the hook."

Major Sedin and Captain Sur didn't speak.

Colonel Wrangel cleared his throat delicately. "Comrade General, it is well known that Dr. Borsilinskow is a very close friend of Wladimir Aleksandr Krasnoyarsk, the president of the Acadamy of Sciences, and that Krasnoyarsk is very close to the First Secretary himself. Need I remind you, Comrade General, that the situation could become very critical for us."

"Comrade, the situation is already critical," Vershensky said in a slow and terrible voice. "It's bad enough that a dangerous kill-expert even knew that Zemlya II existed, but for us to have captured him and then let him slip through our fingers is unforgivable. The only

95

thing that will save our necks is that one of the scientists helped the Death Merchant escape."

"The center can't hold us responsible!" Major Sedin said.

Colonel Wrangel stared thoughtfully into his cup. "It's a tricky situation." He looked up at General Vershensky. "If Doctor Borsilinskow's complaints get to First Secretary Brezhnev—"

"Comrade, what's the matter with you?" Vershensky interrupted in a very sharp voice. "Your memory is worse than that of an old peasant. Have you forgotten that Zemlya II is one of First Secretary Brezhnev's pet projects? What do you think he will say when he learns that a trusted scientist murdered three agents and helped the Death Merchant escape. All of you, stop to think for a moment! Who cleared the scientists with security checks? Whose responsibility was it?"

Captain Tur looked at Major Sedin, and both men smiled. Colonel Wrangel took a sip of tea, his eyes two pools of delight over the rim of the cup.

"Yes, it was the center who checked them out!" Major Sedin said happily. "They'll have to do a lot of explaining to the Kremlin, won't they?"

The telephone on the desk rang.

General Vershensky picked up the receiver. "Yes," he growled.

His three officers watched him nod and saw his fleshy face grow tight with tension.

"All right, Captain Molody," Vershensky said. "Call back the moment he is dead or captured."

He hung up the phone, breathing heavily through his nose.

"Captain Molody has sent men into the armory," he said. "The Death Merchant will soon be our prisoner, or dead. It has to be one or the other."

"Unless he decided to commit suicide by blowing up the arsenal," Major Sedin said, as if talking to himself.

Very deliberately, General Vershensky crushed his cigarette in an ashtray.

"In that case, Comrade, our worries will still be over . . ."

Chapter Eight

The key to success lies more in attitude than aptitude, which is one of the reasons why the Death Merchant remained alive and healthy. In the business of death he had more than enough talent, and in any emergency he exhibited a frame of mind and firmness of purpose that got him through safely.

Hearing the cartridges roll on the steps, he knew the Russians were creeping up toward the second level, and he reacted like a well-oiled machine. He switched a Stechkin to full automatic and ran to that corner of the room where a wall protected him from the stairs, the top of the steps being on the other side of the wall. "Yes, sir," he mumbled, "it's death that gives meaning and purpose to life." He thrust the machine pistol around the corner of the wall, pointed the muzzle downward, and pulled the trigger.

The machine pistol roared, nine hot slugs streaming from the weapon and striking six screaming Russians who had been creeping up the steps in two-man teams, one team behind the other. Only five step's away from the top of the stairs, the first two KGB agents caught slugs in the chest and tumbled backward, their falling clearing a path for the slugs which stabbed the second team of pig farmers a hundredth of a second later. The last two KGB security slobs tried to drop on the steel steps, but a 9mm broke one man's skull like an eggshell, and caught the other man just above the right ear. Bleeding their brains out all over themselves, the two goons sagged and became Corpse Town's newest residents.

Below, on the first floor of the armory, the other KGB boys reacted instinctively. They dove for cover, flattening themselves behind and to the side of crates of pistols, submachine guns, hand grenades, and other equipment, each man terrified, each man wondering if the terrible

Death Merchant might decide to commit suicide and take them with him. It would only take one slug, just one bullet into one block of nitrostarch.

Huddled down by one side of the wrecked sub-shuttle car, Anatoly Kuznestov, the officer in charge, spoke into the walkie-talkie in his hand, his voice frantic. "Captain Molody, we got into the armory as you can see, but somehow the Death Merchant—he's upstairs—spotted the teams and opened fire when they were on the stairs. Tudin, Udalov, Kiktek, Gergel, Degtyarov, and Azarov are dead. What are your orders, Comrade Captain?"

"Wait five minutes and see what he does," came back Yegenni Molody's hard voice. "Then send more teams up after him. There is no other way. First, ask him to surrender. Do you understand?"

"Yes, but Comrade, if he doesn't surrender, and if a stray bullet should get to the explosives or even the hand grenades down here, we'll all be killed. The whole dome will go up," Kuznestov replied nervously.

"You are using small arms only, and the inside of the crates are lined with polychrome plastic," Molody's angry voice jumped out of the walkie-talkie. "All of you are safe enough. Even so, we have to risk it. Damn it, Anatoly! If we don't capture that son of a bitch, we'll all end up patrolling some little village in the middle of nowhere. Now get him. That's an order! Don't phone me back until he's either dead or captured."

"Yes, sir," Kurznestov muttered. He switched off the unit and looked at his wrist watch as the men around him, their weapons trained on the stairs, looked gloomily at him. The thought of being blown to bits was not appealing to them.

"You heard Captain Molody," Kuznestov said, looking and sounding like the star attraction at his own funeral.

The other men slowly nodded.

Ah, comrades, that crazy *Amerikanski* will never surrender," Marat Luda said. "Never . . ."

Upstairs, the Death Merchant shoved another magazine into the Stechkin automatic he had just emptied down the stairs, listened for a moment, then ran back to the box of nitrostarch he had opened and swiftly but cautiously removed the fifty one-pound blocks, stacking them behind another crate. He next removed the bags from his hips, jammed both Stechkin machine pistols into his waistband, picked up the empty box by one of its rope handles, and went back to the corner of the wall next to the stairs.

The tactics of the Russians had not surprised him. What else could the dumb corn pickers do but come up around the sides of the windowless armory and slip through the gaps between the crumpled walls and the doors. By God, there should be a law against such stupidity. Even for Slavic pig farmers!

Camellion was checking the two Vitmorkin machine pistols when he heard a loud and highly nervous voice call up to him: "Death Merchant. This is your last chance to surrender. We will give you five minutes. No more!"

Thinking that if it weren't for Death, the Great Leveler, life would be empty and without purpose, Richard chuckled and returned the two Vitmorkin machine pistols to the holsters of the belt buckled around his waist. As a crooked smile crept across his mouth he picked up the empty explosives box and checked to make sure the hasp was securely fastened. He didn't want the lid to fly open.

Now I'll shake the vodka out of those cornpone patsies!

He picked up the empty box by one of its rope handles.

"What's five minutes compared to eternity?" he shouted, leaning close to the end of the wall. "I'm going to blow up this whole damn dome and take you with me! This box of nitrostarch should do it! Here, catch!"

With one quick motion, he pitched the empty wooden box around the corner of the wall, grinned, and pulled the two Stechkins from his belt as he heard the box bang loudly down the steps.

All right, stupid! Start earning your half a million tax-free bucks!

Anatoly Kuznestov, and the other Russians, hearing Camellion's pronouncement of dooms day, became paralyzed with stark, naked fear. The box, tumbling down the steps, convinced them that he meant what he had said, and that they were as good as dead. Falsely assuming that the box was filled with blocks of explosives and that a severe enough jar would touch all of them off, the security agents threw themselves flat, covered their heads with their arms and tried to pray!

Right behind the box, racing down the steps, came Camellion, his feet pounding on the steps; and by the time Anatoly Kuznestov and the other agents realized that the box was not going to explode from impact, and tried to rear up from the floor, Camellion was at the bottom of the steps, the Stechkin machine pistols roaring.

"The yankee spy tricked us!" Igor Oos yelled, and tried to swing his own Stechkin in Camellion's direction. He should have stayed down. A 9mm hit him in the mouth, tore out his tongue, and blew away the back of his thick neck. Stone dead, Oos fell forward in a spray of blood. He had been right. The Death Merchant had tricked all of them, and the entire joke was on the KGB. They were going to die, not by one tremendous explosion, but by burning 9mm steel.

The Death Merchant had the edge. Not only had he taken the Russians by surprise, but during those few seconds while the Russians were pinned down by his savage fire, he had jumped behind several stacks of crates filled with AK-47 assault rifles.

Disorganized both by fear and surprise, the KGB agents were at a disadvantage, in that they tried to find better cover and zero in on the dreaded Death Merchant at the same time. One man, in trying to escape the thick flood of red flowing out of the first agent Camellion had burned, leaned out too far and exposed himself. He yelled and spun when one of Camellion's bullets banged him in the shoulder, but he barely felt the second 9mm, which zipped through the side of his neck, cut his carotid artery, tore out the other side, and buried itself in the side of a crate across the room. The man gurgled loudly and fell, bleeding twice as much as the first agent Camellion had iced.

Anatoly Kuznestov, Marat Luda, and another agent remained down by one side of the wrecked sub-shuttle car. Across from them, but six feet up ahead, two more

100

agents were huddled against crates of hand grenades, both scared stiff, both afraid that if they engaged the Death Merchant in a shooting match, one of his slugs might accidentally get through the polychrome plastic sheeting and detonate the entire crate, then the entire building. A little farther away, but on the other side, were Esfir Yuryn and Vesvolod Gamow, both of whom were safe enough as long as they remained behind the stack of crates filled with RPG-7 rocket launchers.

Twenty-five feet away was the incredible Death Merchant, getting damned impatient and tired of the whole business. The pig farmers are pinned down—*but so am I!*

He thought of a trick he had used numerous times in the past. The same ruse just might work this time, but only if they hadn't noticed that, other than the two Stechkins in his hands, he was wearing machine pistols in hip holsters.

Richard studied his position. The crates behind which he stood were almost seven feet long, with a two-foot gap between the ends of the crates opposite Camellion and the next line of stacked containers. Why not? Why not give it a try? Anyhow, now was the ideal time. He had only a couple of shells left in each Stechkin.

Yeah, go ahead and do it! In one quick motion, he thrust both Stechkins around the side of the crate on his side and pulled the triggers. There were three quick shots, then the firing pins struck empty chambers. The two machine pistols were empty. To get around the possibility that the hog callers hadn't heard the clicks because of the echo of the shots, Richard released the slides, their snapping back into a normal position recocking both weapons. Again, Camellion thrust the weapons around one of the crates and pulled the triggers. Again there were two loud clicks, so audible that Anatoly Kuzhestov and the two men with him, by the car, heard them.

"He's out of ammunition. Let's get him!" Oos and Aleksei Bykob, the man with him, jumped up and charged in the direction of the Death Merchant, Oos firing a standard Tokarev pistol, Bykob armed with a Makarov automatic. Ahead of them, equally as positive of victory, Esfir Yuryn and Vesvolod Gamow also lost all sense of caution, leaped to their feet, and started dashing toward the crates behind which, so they assumed, the Death Merchant was helpless.

Anatoly Kuznestov had a greater sense of self-preservation.

Wait, wait!" he yelled. "It might be a trick on Camellion's part!"

By then, however it was too late. The four agents, all firing at one end of the crates, had almost reached the Death Merchant.

Back by the side of the sub-shuttle vehicle, Kuznestov motioned impatiently to Marat Luda and Leonid Zazyadko. "Come on! Maybe the Death Merchant is out of shells. If we're fast enough, we can kill the son of a bitch before he can reload." Kuznestov found out how wrong he was when the other four KGBs closed in for what they thought was the kill. Esfir Yuryn and Vesvolod Gamow were only six feet from the crates when Camellion stepped out between the far end of the boxes and the next stack of containers and said, "Tag! You're it!" Then he cut loose with both Vitmorkin submachine pistols, slugs splashing all over the right sides of Esfir Yuryn and Vesvolod Gamow, killing the two men instantly, the way the life of a fly is terminated when its body is broken by a brick!

Realization is faster than physical reflex. Within a tenth of a second, the knowledge of the trap exploded in the minds of Igor Oos and Aleksei Bykob. Both terrified agents tried to dodge the falling corpses of Yuryn and Gamow and at the same time swing to the right to burn out the terrible Death Merchant. An icecube in the center of a blast furnace would have survived a lot longer!

Before either Oos or Bykob could get off a shot at Camellion, his 9mm steel was stabbing all over them. Oos took a slug in the stomach, one in the center of his chest, and a third between the eyes. He died so quickly he didn't even have time to say *God help me!*

Bykob was just as lucky. With his face and the back of his head blown away by 9mm steel, he took a one-way trip to stiff-city. He sagged against the falling Oos, both dead men crashing to the floor as the Death Merchant came forward like an express train. Kuznestov, Luda, and Zazyadko pulled up short and tossed hot death in his direction.

A couple of 9mm bullets passed so close to Richard's head he could hear them cursing in pig farmer language as they burned by and buried themselves in a wooden crate. A 7.62mm Tokarev slug came even closer to his left ear, giving Camellion the feeling someone had touched him with the tip of a feather. Still another hunk of 9mm copper-coated steel skimmed across the top of a holster, leaving a thin tear line on the flap—all of it happening so fast that even God would have had to think three times to deduce what was going on. Kuznestov, Luda, and Zazyadko certainly knew the score! They knew they were going to die!

"Uhhhhhhhh!" moaned Marat Luda. There was only a flash of agony from the 9mm slug which Camellion had put into his belly, and all the tall, dying agent could think of was what his mother had once told him when he was a little boy; that a dream is a truth that never happened. But Luda knew this was real, that he was dying. Then he was dead when the Death Merchant's second bullet stabbed him in the throat, cut apart his Adam's apple, and went merrily on its way via the back of his neck. Gargling on blood, Luda pitched to one side, falling in front of Anatoly Kuznestov, who was so desperate to live that he didn't realize that martyrdom was meant to be shared. Then he didn't realize anything! A 9mm slug hit him in the upper lip, tore out half his upper teeth, and opened a hole in the back of his neck the size of a doorknob. A moment later the Death Merchant's second bullet jumped into Kuznestov's skull and scrambled his brains. A bloody mess of useless flesh, Kuznestov dropped while Leonid Zazyadko, crazed with fear, made the last mistake of his thirty-four years—he tried to dive behind a stack of crates. The Death Merchant helped him along by putting slugs into his right rib cage, and his right temple. The impact knocked the Russian three feet back before he flopped to the floor and lay still—except for his left leg, which continued to twitch for half a dozen seconds.

Camellion felt like cursing! Either the new Russian Vitmorkin machine pistols weren't worth a damn—*or else I'm losing my touch*! Every one of his 9mm Vitmorkin slugs had been off by several inches. Worse, he had aimed for Kuznestov's chest and had hit the dummy in the head! By God, that was even worse than having Richard Nixon as president! Why if Vallie West had witnessed such poor marksmanship, he'd still be laughing—*and advising me to retire!*

Dashing forward, Camellion wished he had his S&W Magnum revolvers with him. No, the big revolvers wouldn't do. What he now needed were weapons that were at the pinnacle of efficiency and the ultimate in power. There was only one kind of handgun for such a job—the sophisticated Auto-Mag, or automatic Magnum, the only Magnum pistol in the world, manufactured in .41, .44, and .357 calibers. *The most powerful handgun on the whole damn planet! Just right for knocking off pig farmers!*

The Death Merchant made up his mind. If he ever reached the United States, he would make some changes in his fire-power. When he went out on the next mission for Uncle Sam, he'd have two .44 Automags with him. *The model 200 International is just what I need.*

Only ten feet from the sub-shuttle car he detected subtle movement on the opposite side of the vehicle, between the ends of the wrecked doors and the ends of the far front wall. *Fudge!* Changing his course to a running zigzag, Camellion cut loose with the two Vitmorkin machine pistols in his hands, the two 9mm slugs hitting a Russian who had one foot in the space. The KGB security man cried out loudly in pain, dropped, and died. The two agents behind him turned and retreated to an igloo to one side of the armory building.

Reaching the front of the sub-shuttle car, Camellion dropped to the floor and looked around the right front tire. Well, well! Five feet away, staring back at him, was a youthful-looking pig farmer, his cheeks all pink and freshly scrubbed.

"Ho, ho, ho!" grinned Camellion, then blew the man's head off.

Richard jumped up, ran to the side of the car, leaned

down, grabbed the small suitcase of electrical timers from the front seat, then moved to the end of the wall and looked through the gap. He couldn't see a single Russian; yet he knew they were out there, even though they might be scared out of their vodka!

As usual, time was not on his side. It never was. The hell with it! He still had to do what he had to do! With a Vitmorkin machine pistol in one hand the suitcase in the other, he ran back up the steps to the second level, put the suitcase on top of a stack of nitrostarch boxes, and ran back down the stairs. This time he had the wrecking bar in one hand.

Camellion glanced again at both spaces between the ends of the doors and the ends of the walls, and once again checked under the sub-shuttle car. Satisfied that Molody and his men were trying to decide what to do, Richard went over to a crate of RPG-7 rocket launchers and pried off the top boards, after which he removed one of the foot-long bazookalike launchers and went to work on a case several feet away.

Five minutes later, he had the RPG-7 launcher and ten of its shells and fuses to match by one of the gap-spaces in the front wall. Calmly he screwed the fuses into the nose of the shells, and placed a shell on the cradle of the launcher.

He got to his feet, leaned close to the gap, and shouted very loudly, "Captain Molody! I'm going to do you and what's left of your men a favor! I suggest you listen!"

Comrade Molody's voice floated back from around the front of the blue igloo which was actually the escape-to-the-surface diving chamber: "I'm listening, Death Merchant!"

"I know that all of you are only doing your duty," Camellion shouted. "I don't want to kill you needlessly. Every man in here is dead. They interrupted me before I could set off the nitrostarch upstairs. Now I'm giving you a final chance. You've got ten minutes to get inside the escape chamber before I send a rocket shell into the explosives. I think we're all as good as dead, but you might survive the blast in the chamber and float to the surface when the dome falls in. And I give you my word I won't kill any man who exposes himself on the roof when he climbs into the bell. But everything is going, starting right now!

Camellion picked up the rocket launcher and its shell and aimed the crosshairs at the igloo thirty-five feet in front, and to the right, of the armory. Because of the narrow gap, he could see only the left rear corner of the building, but that's all he needed. Something else he needed was luck. He hoped the concussion wouldn't touch off the blocks of nitrostarch, which was stacked on the upper floor, only ten feet above his head. If it did, the resulting big bang would be the last sound he heard on earth.

He sighted in on the corner and pulled the trigger of the striker mechanism. There was a loud *whoosh,* a streak of red flame three feet long, and the rocket hit the igloo, exploding with a muffled roar. Just as Richard had hoped, the concrete and steel mesh absorbed most of the force, the walls and ceiling acting as a kind of sponge. For only a fraction of a second, walls and roof seemed to expand slightly, as if the dying building were inhaling its last breath. Slowly then the rear wall, and the wall on the right hand side, fell inward like a fat old man falling drunk into bed. Camellion heard a couple of short screams and saw a thick cloud of dust rise slowly over the area. That was all.

"Camellion!" screamed Captain Molody, his voice frantic with fear. "At least give us a chance to get inside the chamber, please!"

Well now, the pig farmers are falling for it! Camellion answered, shouting, "I said that everything is going to go. And if you don't start getting into the escape chamber, I'll blast it next! Do what you want! I'll tell you something else, Molody. If there is anyone in the three igloos behind me, you'd better get them out. Those three igloos are so close to this building, they'll be turned into fine dust by the explosion. You go into the chamber last, and call out to me. That way I'll know all of you are in. Then, old buddy, my world ends. So will yours unless you're damned lucky!"

"You said ten minutes!" Molody screamed back. "It won't even take us five minutes. All my men are up

106

front, here in front of the chamber. And five or six are in another igloo, the one in front to your right!"

"You'd better get 'em out! In a few more minutes I'm going to put a shell into that igloo!"

Camellion listened. He heard someone barking orders from the front of the escape igloo, but could not hear what was being said or who had been shouting. He did see the result, when men began running across the area to his right, from the front of the igloo on the right to the front of the huge escape-chamber.

Ah ha! Camellion saw a man's head appear by the far side of the entrance hatch in the center of the slightly domed roof. The man stared straight at the armory for a long moment, then turned and looked behind him, as though he might be listening to someone urging him on.

Hurry up, stupid, Camellion whispered to himself. *I'm not going to burn you out . . . not yet. I want all of you in there.*

Confident that the Death Merchant was not going to blow his head off, the Russian moved higher on the roof until the entire length of his body was exposed. One of the "sun-bathers," he still wore only his shorts. He started spinning the lock-wheel, and soon had the hatch cover thrown back as more Russians appeared on the roof. Three of the Russians wore gray clothes— work clothes—and Richard assumed they were the men, the technicians, who had been unloading the oxygen bottles.

The Death Merchant counted the Russians as they disappeared through the hatch. Down they went, as if Sammael, the angel of death, were chasing them. He was, only they didn't know how close he was to spitting on their Slavic souls.

However, the twenty-eighth man did not get into the hatch immediately. A pudgy-looking hay raker in a light blue uniform shirt and pants to match, he stood up straight, cupped his hands to his mouth and shouted, Death Merchant! This is Captain Molody. I am the last man. But once more I urge you to surrend—"

"Get in and lock the hatch, dead man!" Camellion yelled with mock anger. "I'm going to blow up the nitrostarch! Get your butt in there, buster!"

Molody almost fell down the ladder of the hatch in his haste to get inside the escape chamber. Camellion couldn't help but grin when he saw the wheel on top of the hatch spin as Molody locked the chamber from the inside.

Camellion put a shell into the RPG-7 launcher and thought of a passage from the Bible, his favorite book of myth and masochism, sin and sadism—"He leadeth me beside still waters." *But the Old Testament, the world's first Mein Kampf, was the biggest con of all. According to this "inspired" nonsense, the Almighty never intended Himself to be the god of all people, but only the god of His "chosen" people. Naturally who was "chosen" was a matter of human judgment. There was a time, too, that god was completely unknown until He revealed Himself to Moses, who didn't know who He was! Uh huh, and what about the deal of the Heavenly Boss telling Moses that He had hardened Pharoah's heart, "that I may show these signs of mine" and so that Mr. Moses can tell his son and grandson "how I have made sport of the Egyptians and what I have done among them; that you may know that I am the Lord." Some sport! This "sport" consisted of murdering all of the Egyptians' first-born children, so that "there was not a house where one was not dead."*

Richard picked up the rocket launcher and aimed it dead center on the rear wall of the blue igloo which was nothing but a hollow metal ball enclosed by four walls.

"He leadeth me beside still waters." I'm going to lead all of you straight into Deathland. I don't have a choice! I can't risk letting you ice me out when I go for the tractor.

Camellion pulled the trigger. A whoosh! A bright streak of flame, and a muffled roar when the exploding fuse sent the armor-piercing shell boring through the concrete and steel mesh wall. The explosion of the shell inside the diving chamber was a hollow *whoommmmm,* similar to a firecracker going off inside a steel barrel.

The Death Merchant felt sorry for the Russians trapped inside the escape bell, their screams cut short by the second shell he sent in a moment later. Silence! Nothing but blue flame drifting lazily upward.

Was the blue igloo to the right actually empty, or had Molody lied? *If he did lie, then the jokers inside are playing against a stacked deck!*

Several minutes later, the igloo to Camellion's right was a smoking mess of rubble. Another couple of minutes and Camellion, fully loaded Vitmorkins in his hands, was running in a wild angle to the second igloo to one side of the armory. He threw open the door and charged inside. The building was empty. He went to the other buildings, one after another—the three to the rear of the armory and the one on the other side, to the left. All four buildings were deserted. Captain Molody had been telling the truth: all the KGB agents had been in the escape chamber.

Richard raced back to the armory, grabbed the suitcase of electric fuses, and ran to the place in the second level where he had stashed the fifty one-pound bars of nitrostarch. Worried that by some strange quirk of fate he wouldn't be able to make contact with Doctor Raya Dubanova in Dome 1, he fitted a timer each onto a bar of the explosive, almost tenderly pushing the prongs through the oiled brown paper into the putty-like material, and setting the timers to maximum, two hours— 120 minutes, or 7,2000 seconds to detonation, to dooms day.

There existed the possibility that someone from another dome might discover the primed bars and neutralize them by pulling out the timers. Camellion didn't dare to venture a guess as to what could happen after he blasted his way into the control center. Sending rocket shells through both locks of the tube between Domes 1 and 2 might automatically release the locks in all the connecting tubes, in which case KGB personnel from other sections of Zemlya II could pour into Dome 2 and reach the armory.

To insure the success of at least one big bang, Richard went to the last row of stacked cartons by the wall and chose a box in the top center, one so high that he almost had to stand on tiptoe to reach it. He placed the box on the floor, unfastened the hasp, and opened the carton, throwing back the wooden lid. Soon he had attached timers to three bars and had returned the closed box to its original position in the row. If KGB agents did come to the armory and find the other fifty one-pound bars, it was likely that they would be satisfied and not consider it necessary to check the rest of the explosives, crate by crate. Then again, they might. There was simply no way to tell.

Feeling a glow of satisfaction, Camellion next went to the corner of the wall by the top of the stairs, slipped on his two shoulder bags, and picked up the vulgar-looking Dragunov submachine gun.

Suppose Raya Dubanova wasn't in the control dome? Suppose he missed her? *If I do, I'm dead! I don't know how to operate one of the baby subs!*

But he refused to think of failure as he ran down the stairs, slipped through the left hand gap in the front wall, and hurried to the sub-shuttle tractor which was to the left of the wrecked igloo containing the escape chamber. His cautious approach was unnecessary. All the Russians were stone dead, and the Death Merchant was alone in the dome, his only companions the sweet stink of death and the billions of tons of water overhead. That was another of his prime worries—the water. Just suppose that when he blasted the round lock at the end of the tube, the concussion wrecked the tube, or weakened the lower part of the dome into which the tube was built. In either case, the Arctic Ocean would be the victor.

Keeping the submachine gun handy, Camellion removed the pin hooking the half unloaded wagon to the tractor and climbed into the driver's compartment in the rear of the vehicle which reminded him of a scaled-down diesel locomotive; the difference was that this "locomotive" had eight big rubber-tired wheels, lacked a cowcatcher, and was not meant to run on tracks.

Camellion drove the tractor to the front of the armory igloo, went inside the building, and raced back to the second level, thinking of the similarities between organized religion and world communism as he pulled back the lids of two boxes, each of which contained ten five-pound bars of nitrostarch.

Brothers of sadism, both Christianity and Communism demanded blind faith and blind obedience. Like Christianity, Communism was one giant monastic order in which the individual was ordered to lose his intellectual identity and submerge himself into the will of the group. Both systems praised sacrifice and elevated misery to the position of a virtue. Both systems, with their symbols and slogans, were as useless as prayer and as moronic as mysticism! It was the same with most systems, throughout the history of man. Whether it was the cross or the crescent, the swastika or the hammer and sickle, each system elevated stupidity, condoned brutality—either in the name of God or for the good of the state—and insisted that its warped worshippers change themselves into unthinking and unfeeling fanatics! Ireland, with its religious war and censorship of the press, was a good example. A double truckload of bovine excrement! Two big bulging barrels of bullshit! And triple fudge!

Hoping that Raya Dubanova had assembled the electric timers properly, the Death Merchant checked his work. Two five-pound bars of nitrostarch in each box were timed to go off in an hour and forty-five minutes. Enough explosive to blow five-hundred pig farmers to hell! But everybody kills for money, one way or another—*My way is only more direct and less painful.*

Richard closed the lids, fastened the hasps securely, and picked up a box in each hand by its twisted rope handle. With the submachine gun slung over one shoulder, he carried the two boxes of nitrostarch down to the tractor and placed them in the driver's compartment, shoving them in the tool locker on one side of the bucket seat. His next move was to put the rocket launcher and ten shells on the floor of the driver's compartment, after which he got into the seat and drove the tractor to the end of the tube that linked the dome with the control center, bringing the vehicle to a halt forty feet from the round vault-like lock.

He put a rocket shell into the launcher, put the pad on his shoulder, and aimed at the shiny metal lock, centering the crosshairs about six feet from the floor.

Now I'll find out whether I live or die!

111

He pulled the trigger, then ducked down into the driver's compartment!

Wooommmmm! The rocket shell exploded inside the twenty-two-inch-thick hollow lock-door, the blast sending twisted jigsaw pieces of hot metal flying outward, many of which struck the rounded side of the dome and the top and the sides of Camellion's tractor, hitting the vehicle with a sharp ringing sound.

The Death Merchant licked his dry lips and studied the lock. The rocket shell had blown a gaping hole in the metal, the edges of the hole curled and smoking, a yawning aperture almost, but not quite, large enough to admit the tractor. Yet apparently there was no damage to the circular rim where the mouth of the tube was secured to the opening in the dome.

Camellion looked at the dome itself. He couldn't detect a single scratch, much less an out-and-out crack.

He put another rocket shell into the launcher, and this time aimed to the left of the yawning hole. There was another *Wooommmmm,* and more dislodged metal rained down on the area and up against the polychrome plastic dome. This time the rocket shell had done the job. The round lock had been three-fourths demolished, and now there was ample room for the tractor to pass through.

The Death Merchant saw something else: there was a crack in the dome, beginning at the top of the connecting rim and moving upward to the left at a sixty-degree angle, like a thirty-foot-long streak of lightning.

Let's get the hell out of here!

Chapter Nine

Sammael, the angel of death, is always impersonal, never playing favorites, not even with those who assist him in the taking of life and in the dispensing of oblivion, not even with those who are kill-masters, such as Richard Joseph Camellion.

The Death Merchant took another thoughtful look at the lightning like crack in the dome and, muttering "Not yet, you son of a bitch," started the engine of the tractor, drove the vehicle straight through the jagged hole in the lock, and brought it to a halt twenty-five feet from the opposite lock at the other end of the tube.

He had no illusions as to what was waiting for him on the other side of the lock, any more than he could delude himself about his chances for survival if the crack in the side of Dome 2 gave way and the ocean started to rush in. If that happened, his life expectancy would decrease to about five minutes at maximum. He was in even more danger than the Russians in Domes 4 The personnel in those domes could always float to the surface of the ocean in escape chambers.

Camellion couldn't see what was on the other side of the lock, not that it mattered. From his position in the connecting tube he could see partially into the control dome, but only in a hazy, diffused sort of way because of the twelve-inch thickness of both the tube's walls and the dome of the control center. Another obstacle was the water between the tube and the dome; yet Camellion could detect vague shapes of various buildings, looking murky through the glass of faintly luminous water.

Wanting to get into the control dome as quickly as possible, he put a rocket shell into the receiver of the launcher, aimed at the lock twenty feet in front of him, and pulled the trigger, the resulting explosion pounding on his eardrums as he ducked down, reverberating within the length and width of the tube, along with the wang-wangs of metal shreds striking the front of the sub-shuttle tractor.

Camellion didn't even bother to look at the lock before he put another shell in the launcher, raised the bazooka like weapon, and aimed it again at the lock. He got a brief glimpse of a huge jagged rent in the center of the lock, aimed a foot below the bottom of the gash, and pulled the trigger.

After the shattering explosion, he looked up over the edge of the dashboard, saw that there was now room for

113

the sub-shuttle tractor to pass through, and spotted some of the cars lined up on the other side of the huge, smoking hole, men in uniform moving behind the cars.

We'll have to do something about those birds, won't we?

He put another shell into the launcher.

In the control dome, on the other side of the sub-shuttle barrier, the KGB agents waited uneasily. Captain Paul Yubishkanonavitch ran up and down the line yelling, "Get ready, Comrades! He'll be coming through the lock in a moment!

He stopped in the middle of the line, next to the two-man crew behind the ZPU-2 machine gun. He leaned down and tapped the gunner on the shoulder, "Boris, don't fire until you see him clearly. Then cut him to pieces."

Boris Linsayko nodded. Yes, but what do we do if he starts using rocket shells after he's inside? How do we fight them, Comrade Captain?"

Yubishkanonavitch frowned at Linsayko, wishing he hadn't asked the question. "It's not likely that he will continue to use those shells. He can't, unless he he stays with the tractor. If he comes through with the tractor, you can stop it easily with your machine gun. Don't worry, Comrade Linsayko. The Death Merchant is as good as dead."

Yubishkanonavitch patted Linsayko on the shoulder, then moved down the line, checking to make sure that each man was in position. The procedure saved his life. Just as he reached the edge of the line that was only fifty feet from the side of the dome itself, the Death Merchant's third shell *whooshed* through the hole in the lock-door and hit the car in the center of the barricade, the one that was mounted with the ZPU-2 14.5mm heavy machine gun. With a loud roar and a blinking bright red flash of flame, the rocket shell exploded, the terrible blast tearing the shuttle car apart and killing instantly the two machine gunners. The big ZPU-2 went flying through the air, and so did the two corpses of Laurenti Agrafenin and Boris Linsayko, Agrafenin without a head, Linsayko minus his left arm and right leg.

In that same instant, other agents were kicked into Corpse-town! Part of the metal driver's wheel hit a man in the face, the ragged end driving itself upward into his brain while pieces of the blown apart car stabbed other agents. A three-foot length of the car's siding sliced into Sergei Sabotka's chest. He gasped like a man who has just discovered his wife in bed with another woman, staggered crazily to one side, and fell against Josef Bilorous, who was trying to remove a jagged piece of aluminum that had buried itself in his belly. Bilorous failed, just as Sabotka succeeded only in dying. Both men fell heavily, Sabotka with metal sticking out of his chest and back, Bilorous with his hands wrapped around the foot of aluminum buried in his gut.

The explosion had triggered instant butchery! Yuri Sitnikov screamed like a panther when the ZPU-2 crashed back down, hit him in the right arm, and snapped it at the elbow. He was still more lucky than Andrew Pov, who sank to one knee, his hands pressed tightly over a bloody face that had lost much of its nose to a razor like piece of metal which had sheared half of it off.

Captain Yubishkanonavitch, knocked down by the terrific concussion but otherwise unharmed, picked himself up and tried hard not to vomit when he saw the bloody head of Agrafenin lying only a few feet away.

He stared around him in horror. Seven agents were dead. A dozen more were wounded. The rest, although unhurt, were dazed.

His mind in a panic, his ears still roaring, Yubishkanonavitch screamed, "Get the damned assassin! He's coming through!" when he saw the tractor coming through the hole in the blasted lock at forty m.p.h. He stooped down to pick up an AK-47 assault rifle, the move saving his life for the second time within seventy-four seconds. As he leaned down, the Death Merchant swung the tractor sharply to the right and opened fire with the Dragunov submachine gun, holding the weapon in his left hand and turning the small steering wheel with his right.

If Yubishkanonavitch had been standing erect, he would have caught a 7.62mm slug in the chest. As it was, the bullet passed over his head and back and caught Nicholas Kivv in his left arm. Kivv cried out, grabbed his arm, and dropped to the floor, cursing in a loud voice. But it was die-time for three other political security agents of the KGB. Arkadi Peziz got steel-stabbed in the side of the neck, the 7.62mm slug tearing out his throat as it bored all the way through and caught Vadim Gorky just below his right lower jaw. Gurgling blood and bone chips, both candidates for Corpse-land spun like wobbly tops and tilted toward the floor, falling only ten feet from Stepan Pallid, who had been baptized with a bullet in his brain, and Aleksei Sedov, who was sinking with slugs in his hip and side.

"Fire, you idiots! Kill him!" screamed Yubishkanona-vitch. He jumped to one side of a shuttle car and swung the AK-47 toward the racing tractor.

An angry and worried Richard Camellion had not anticipated the second group of slobs, but there they were, 175 feet ahead of him, behind a makeshift barracade ringing the long line of air compressors, which filled the warm air with a loud pounding as their pistons forced air into the overhead induction pipes.

As the sub-shuttle tractor approached, the guards at one end of the enclosure opened fire, sending a hurricane of burning steel at Camellion. Rifle and submachine gun slugs stung the grilled high front end of the tractor, which Camellion, crouching low in the driver's compartment, was swerving back and forth. More hot steel burned over his head through the top part of the driver's cab, some only a scant few inches above his head. Because of the distance, many of the rifle and submachine gun bullets bounced off the tractor, but as the vehicle drew closer, some of the steel ripped through the metal and found its way into the forward section of the battery compartment, shorting out the batteries.

The tractor began slowing down as Camellion turned it toward the right and headed toward the side of the dome thirty-five feet away. More 7.62mm steel stabbed the sides of the tractor, coming from both Captain

Yubishkanonavitch's group—what remained of it—and the agents surrounding the air compressors. Now and then a bullet zinged into the tool compartment behind the driver's seat and thudded dully into the two crates of nitrostarch.

Camellion was not concerned: the slugs had lost most of their force in tearing through the metal sides of the tractor, and by the time they bored through the hard wood of the two crates and struck the polychrome plastic protecting the bars of explosive, their power was practically nil.

Placing the tractor where he wanted it was another problem, and before slugs killed the last battery, it was all Richard could do to turn the vehicle around and park it horizontally to, and ten feet from, the six-foot-high protective mesh fence, which was only five feet from the side of the dome itself. The destruction of Zemlya II was now a ninety-nine percent certainty unless the KGB discovered the two crates of nitrostarch in the tool compartment. When the nitrostarch exploded, the blast would tear a hundred foot hole in that side of the dome. The Arctic Ocean would do the rest, flooding the entire control center within minutes and destroying the air compressors. With the air pressure gone, Domes 2, 3, 4, and 5 would collapse, even if the tons of explosive in the armory didn't detonate. Zemlya II was doomed.

And so am I! How do I stay alive, find Raya Dubanova, reach a radio and call the Albacore for help, get to the lock-out chamber with her, and—he consulted his wristwatch—escape with her in a little less than an hour and a half?

Mrs. Camellion's eldest son considered the fine fix he had gotten himself into. This was certainly one helluva way to make a living, but it was more acceptable than leading a normal life—and it was all tax free.

Calmly he studied his position. A hundred feet to his left was Captain Yubishkanonavitch's group. Not quite seventy-five feet to his right were the KGB meatballs protecting the air compressors. Fifteen feet behind him was the side of the dome, the watery grave of the Arctic Ocean beyond. Spread out in front of him, in all its Communist glory, was the interior of the control dome.

Dead ahead, fifty feet, was the smoke detection and air purification station, a three-story deal with a spider-web of pipes, one of which stretched out to the connecting tube, then moved onward to the other four domes.

Next to the s.d.a.p. station, to his right, was the water purification station, whose machines extracted salt from the ocean water. The main induction pipe, eight feet in diameter, led to the other side of the dome. Mounted on twenty-foot-high steel X braces, the pipe cradled in the "V" portion of the X.

Further ahead was the general meeting hall, to its left the gymnasium. To the left of the gymnasium was the larger-than-most blue igloo that was KGB headquarters. Richard was positive of the location, having implanted in his mind its position in the dome when Comrade Yubishkanonavitch and his five goons had first taken him to General Vershensky's office, and later when the guards had taken him to Dome 3.

The Death Merchant was also positive of the location of the communications building. It had to be the small blue igloo cube next to the two-story KGB headquarters, the proof being the CETI-4 type antenna whose four wires rose from one side of the igloo, straight up through the main dome to the surface of the ocean where an antenna-buoy bobbed, held in place by a large sea anchor and a loose mooring wire secured to the ocean's floor.

There were several sub-shuttle cars parked to one side of the communications igloo, and half a dozen more lined up in front of KGB headquarters.

Far to the right of the meeting hall was a machine that the Death Merchant had read about, but had never seen before—a giromill (from cyclogiro windmill), a vertical-axis windmill, with forty-foot-high blades that were airfoils, like the wings of an airplane. In front of the giromill was the kind of fan that was usually reserved for a wind tunnel, the twenty-five-foot blades shielded in a heavy mesh screen and blowing on the giromill, which in turn furnished the power for the electric generating station forty feet away.

With bullets bouncing off, and into, the sub-shuttle tractor, the Death Merchant did some rapid calculating. He was one-hundred per cent positive that Raya Dubanova had to be somewhere in the control dome. Her car had been ahead of his, and he had seen it go through the connecting tube into Dome 2, and then on into Dome 1. There was just one problem: *Where is she? How do I find her—and stay alive while I'm doing it?*

He had another problem—to his left, on the other side of the dome, 150 feet away, was the round metal lock which opened into the dock section. Here in this vast lock-out chamber were the submarine pens with the all-important "little-boats"—important because without them, Camellion was a dead man. *I'm a corpse anyhow if I don't find Raya Dubanova!*

To get to the "passenger little-boats," Richard was convinced he would have to open the entrance lock with rocket shells, and do it before he left the sub-shuttle tractor. That was the whole damn problem—once the lock was torn apart, would the pressure of the lock-out chamber be lowered to the extent that the water would pour in? Or was the pressure of the entire dome higher than the entry pressure of the water? No use to worry about it! He was certainly damned if he didn't blast the lock!

He put a rocket shell onto the launcher, thrust the tube out the front of the cab, and, ignoring the slugs singing their litany of hate, sighted in on the shiny lock and pulled the trigger. The shell exploded a tenth of a second later.

And so did the left side of the Death Merchant's head as a ricocheting 7.62mm bullet cut through his short brown hair and raked his skull, just enough to make him feel that his head had been caressed by the tip of a red-hot poker. Damn those creeps!

Ignoring the blood creeping down the side of his head, he sent the second shell into the lockdoor, placing it three feet below the first hole. Another big whhhoommmmm, and when the flash of flame and smoke cleared there was an eight-foot gap in what was left of the lock.

Zzzinnggggggggg!!!! The bullet smacked a metal brace

of the canopy over the cab, bounced off, hit a large screw head on the opposite side of the compartment, then slammed into the buckle of one of the bag straps lying across his chest.

That bullet had come from the left! More slugs followed from both the left and the right, the loud whines of metal glancing off metal soon lost within the myriad other sounds filling the control dome.

Richard had had enough of the Russian fig newtons! Time to let the Slavic cookies know who the boss really was. He thrust a rocket shell into the launcher, sighted through the left side of the cab, and sent the missile toward Captain Yubishkanonavitch and what remained of his group. The resulting explosion tore apart five more. As if magically protected, Yubishkanonavitch was unhurt. Enough was enough! Firing wildly at the tractor, he and three men with him retreated, running toward the KGB headquarters cube.

Camellion reloaded the launcher, and this time thrust the tube out the right side of the cab, aiming it at the KGB security boys, who had formed a rectangle around the air compressors with a makeshift barricade. The end facing Camellion was twenty feet from the side of the first compressor, and he knew there was little chance that a shell would damage the machines. What it would do to the boobs behind the seven sub-shuttle cars was something else!

The first shell demolished two cars, throwing frames, hoods, batteries, and tires upward and outward, the thunderous blast ripping apart eight security men and wounding as many more. The wounded and dying were still screaming when the second shell—the last one Camellion had—turned the rest of the line into twisted, smoking steel and broken, bloody bodies. Two men went flying all the way back to the first air compressor, one dummy crashing into the fly-wheel which, in a shower of blood, flung him another twenty feet. He hit the floor, bounced twice, died once, and lay still.

Fate insisted on playing its own grim joke. At the same time that the second rocket shell exploded, three sub-shuttle cars came from the other end of the rectangle, two coming up on one side, one on the other, the shell bursting just as the three vehicles were parallel with the other cars in the front line of the barricade.

The two cars together, although rocked violently by the terrific concussion, managed to survive the blast and continue on their course. The third vehicle ran straight into the worst kind of trouble. A metal canopy from one of the blown apart cars sliced through the air toward the driver's seat.

In that blink of a tense second the KGB agent behind the wheel, seeing the four-foot square of metal coming at him like the blade of guillotine, tried desperately to avoid the canopy by swerving the car out of its path. He tried too hard! He twisted the wheel too sharply and the sub-shuttle car overturned, throwing him and the other five men onto the aluminum flooring of the dome— sending them straight into the submachine gun slugs of the Death Merchant, who had jumped from the tractor and was firing the Dragunov from behind the cab.

"Ring-a-ding-dong, dummies, you'll all dead!" Camellion said lazily, and then the six men were riddled into oblivion, the 7.62mm slugs heaving them into hell with such speed that the devil didn't even have time to send a welcoming committee.

While the agents at the shattered barricade tried to reorganize and recover from shock, the other two sub-shuttle cars, one alongside the other, headed straight for the tractor. The men beside the drivers fired AK-47 assault rifles at the right side of the tractor, the only side they could see. The KGB agents did their best to kill Camellion, who had moved to the left rear side of the sub-shuttle tractor and, grenades in his hands, listened intently to the loud humming of the electric engines, judging the distance of the two cars as their drivers tried to close in on him. He had pulled the pin-rings of the grenades, his hands pressed down on the levers to keep them from exploding.

With a low bitter laugh Richard rolled the two hand grenades underneath the tractor, directing them at the cars when he estimated they could not be more than twenty-five feet away. His timing was almost perfect. One grenade exploded a foot under the car to the left, the burst wrecking the front end and turning the vehicle over on its side, its six terrified occupants tumbling out in a pretzel-like tangle of arms, legs, and automatic weapons.

The Death Merchant had better luck with the second grenade. It detonated underneath the center of the other car, the upward force of the blast turning the metal floor into shrapnel that riddled four KGB goons before the vehicle turned over and dumped them and their three comrades onto the floor of the dome, where they joined the six agents from the other car, who were reaching for their AK's and wondering how long they were going to stay alive.

They didn't have to wonder very long! Danil Komushkin, the driver of one car, was the first man to see the Death Merchant moving back and forth to the right of the tractor, the Stechkin machine pistols roaring in his hands.

Time for pig slaughter! Komushkin, with a 9mm slug in his chest, died at the same time the agent next to him choked out a short scream from the stab of the slug entering his throat. Sinking into a vast, dark pit filled with his own blood, the man never heard the cries of fear from the other agents, who were reaching for automatic rifles or struggling to get to their feet, as they were ripped to pieces by the deadly fire of the Death Merchant.

Boris Misko, half-lying on his side, his left leg broken, gamely tried to trigger off a shot at Camellion, who put a 9mm slug into his face before the Russian could even pull the trigger of his own Tokarev automatic. Hair, chips of bone, and scrambled bits of brain splattered over Peter Chobov, who was cursing, trying not to gag, and at the same time doing his best to swing the muzzle of his AK-47 on a weaving, dodging Camellion. Spotting Chobov's motion, Richard promptly baptized him with two slugs, the first battering his breastbone, tearing through the left ventricle of his heart, and lodging in his spine, the second smashing him in the solar plexus, then going bye-bye out his back, ringing loudly as it ricocheted from the still spinning wheel of an overturned sub-shuttle car.

Memento mori! The KGB agents were well trained and very fast; yet they didn't possess the Death Merchant's sharp instincts; they didn't have his experience and know-how; they weren't kill-experts.

Long ago, Camellion had learned that in a fire-fight you never let yourself get too close to your opponents. When you do, there's too much danger of becoming distracted. If you get too close, you can see a man sweat and watch fear dry out his lips and make his eyes go wild. You lose your objectivity; your concentration starts to wobble. That's when the enemy might kill you.

An experienced kill-master "reads" the enemy the way a veteran performer "reads" an audience. Camellion knew this "audience" was scared stiff! And fear, always a partner to cowardice, is always an extremely dangerous enemy: fear gives an enemy greater speed and often makes him twice as dangerous as he would be if cool under fire. Furthermore, an expert exterminator never, but *never*, watches his enemy, not in the usual sense: he concentrates only on weapons. To Richard Camellion, the KGB agents weren't men; they were only the flesh and blood and bone extensions of their weapons.

Camellion jerked himself to one side, firing both machine pistols, the high velocity slugs hitting Ryurik Bogaty and Aleksei Davidovsky, both of whom had drawn down on Camellion, Bogaty with a SKS carbine, Davodovsky using an AK-47. Bogaty's 7.62mm slug burned very close to Camellion, but the big Russian didn't get the second chance to ice Camellion. His skull popped open like an overripe orange as Richard's two 9mm pieces of steel stabbed into his forehead and scattered his think-tank in assorted directions.

Davidovsky didn't do any better, but he had an excuse. Shrapnel from the flooring of one car had riddled his intestines and he was dying; yet he still managed to fire a burst of AK-47 slugs at Camellion, who jumped to the right and snap-aimed a shot at the Russian. The bullet caught Davidovsky in the open mouth and sent the back of his head flying five feet back against the middle seat of one overturned sub-shuttle car. Looking dumbfounded, as if frozen in wax, Davidovsky pitched forward, falling against Yakov Mokin, who had been blinded in one eye by shrapnel. But Mokin was so filled with burning hatred of Camellion that he didn't notice the pain. He swung his Dragunov submachine gun up at the hated Death Merchant who jumped forward and down almost flat just as Mokin pulled the trigger. The stream of steel death passed over Camellion, hitting the side of the tractor and chopping through the metal. Richard polished off Mokin with the last three cartridges in the Stechkin in his left hand and with two slugs from the machine pistol in his right hand, also killed Ivan Ogiluisin, a very tall Russian who had triggered off two shots at the Death Merchant.

One of Ogiluisin's SKS carbine slugs tore through the top side of the bag containing Camellion's hand grenades. In an instant faster than the speed of light Camellion marveled that he was still alive, which wouldn't have been the case had the 7.62mm bullet hit a hand grenade. As Camellion figured it, the bullet must have passed within a tenth of an inch of the highest grenade in the bag; but still not close enough to open the narrow door to Deathland, unlike Ogiluisin's second piece of steel, which tore through the other bag flopping around on Camellion's other hip. That 7.62 wanged into the edge of a submachine gun magazine, ricocheted off, cut back through the canoprene bag, flew another ten feet and hit the military sight of Jacob Lyudin's SKS carbine, knocking the muzzle a foot to one side.

Mokin, Ogiluisin, and Lyudin died almost as one man. Mokin, hit in the throat, lower chest, and stomach, choked out a big bloody "Uhhh!" and collapsed sideways, the side of his head smacking the already bloody aluminum floor, his eyes wide, staring, and blank.

The Death Merchant arrowed himself to the left, fell prone, and fired three shots, one slug tapping the top of Ogiluisin's head. The sharp-nosed 9mm bullet tore through the Russian's brain, cut through the roof of his mouth, skipped down the long tunnel of his throat, and cut through the length of his body, stopping only when it came to the vicinity of his pelvis. Ogiluisin shuddered and fell flat on his face, a great pool of red widening under his body, while Lyudin went down with a bullet in his stomach, the twisting motion of his body from the impact causing the barrel of the SKS to whip around toward the barricade around the air compressors. Automatic muscular reflex tightened his finger against the trigger, and the muzzle roared out a steam of hot steel toward fourteen KGB gunmen running from the barricade toward the battle. One agent yelled and went down, a bullet in his leg. Another goon cried out, spun around, and crashed down unconscious, his face streaming blood. The other twelve Russians dropped flat—confused, uncertain of who was firing at whom, uncertain of what to do.

Not so with the Death Merchant. He was positive of what he had to do. Spotting the reinforcements, as well as catching the actions of Safar Krimsky and Isim Nereuda, Richard jumped up, dropped his empty Stechkins, and pulled both Vitmorkin machine pistols from their holsters, all the while careful to keep an overturned sub-shuttle car between himself and the dozen agents fifty feet to his right, between him and the barricade. Right now he had other worries.

Isim Nereuda's legs had been riddled with sharp and jagged pieces of the metal flooring from one sub-shuttle car, and he was in agony and weak from loss of blood; nonetheless, he was a fanatical Communist and dedicated KGB officer who was determined to kill the Death Merchant. Nereuda deliberately took a slow and steady aim at Camellion, holding the Vitmorkin with both hands. He pushed himself up three feet and fired at the same moment that Safar Krimsky pulled the trigger of his submachine gun and the Death Merchant threw himself against the side—really the bottom—of an overturned car.

Nereuda's line of burning 9mms passed between Camellion's legs—three inches higher and they would have turned him into a eunuch—while the stream of fire from Krimsky's submachine gun cut within an inch of Richard's left side, one slug tearing through his shirt sleeve and barely raking his elbow. Neither Nereuda nor Krimsky had time to bat their eyes before they were stone dead, riddled by the twin stab of slugs from Camellion's machine pistols.

Nereuda cried out and his body sagged, blood streaming from his mouth, neck, and chest. Two seconds later he was in hell.

In contrast, Safar Krimsky had received three 9mms directly in the face. He fell backward so hard he almost bounced. Where his face had been was only a raw, gaping mess.

There was only one Russian left from the two overturned cars—Josip Zalstoie, who had dislocated his knee when he had been pitched from the first car. Zalstoie had not fired a single shot. First of all, there weren't any automatic weapons within reach of the roly-poly agent. Then, too, his personal religion wouldn't permit him to fight unless the odds were on his side. A devout coward, Zalstoie had no intention of risking his life needlessly; and he didn't want to risk using his Makarov pistol. If he missed, he'd only succeed in drawing Camellion's attention, in getting himself killed. He did the next best thing—he played dead. Now he began to crawl away from the area, moving like a worm toward the smoke detection and air purification station. Since he was moving away from the area, he hoped the Death Merchant wouldn't shoot him in the back.

Camellion didn't. He needed information from the man, but before he could get to Zalstoie, he'd have to take care of the dozen gunmen up ahead. Rather than take time to unsling the Dragunov submachine gun strapped to his back, Camellion moved forward and picked up the Dragunov dropped by Safar Krimsky. Aware that the precious seconds were ticking away, he ran to the end of one overturned sub-shuttle car, dropped to one knee, thrust the barrel around the end of the car, and opened fire. He moved the weapon back and forth, from side to side, raking the KGB boobs who had jumped up from the dome's floor and were running toward him.

Blowing away the pig farmers was as easy as shooting bottles lined up on a fence. Six seconds and twenty-six 9mm slugs later, the Russians were dead meat, their corpses lying in assorted positions on the aluminum floor, a few still kicking and shuddering. They jerked again as Camellion put more slugs into them; then they lay still forever.

Richard reloaded the Dragunov chatter-box, looked around him, then headed across the area toward the smoke detection and air purification station. The pig farmer who had crawled away couldn't have gotten very far.

Josip Zalstoie hadn't! He had managed to reach one corner of the smoke and air station building and to crawl around on the side that the Death Merchant could not see, any more than Zalstoie could see Camellion.

Alone and afraid, Zalstoie heard the savage burst of a Dragunov and suspected that instead of his comrades killing the Death Merchant, it had been the other way around. Would Camellion come after him? No, he concluded, or the terrible *Amerikanski* would have killed him earlier when he had had the opportunity. But suppose Camellion came toward the smoke and air station and happened to spot him? A chill raced over Zalstoie.

Lying against the side of the building, Zalstoie turned to face the direction of the overturned sub-shuttle cars, pulled the Makarov pistol from its holster, and began to wait, his ears filled with the roar of the fan blowing against the giromill.

Perhaps a minute passed. Zalstoie choked out a cry of fear and felt his stomach drop when he felt a hard muzzle press firmly against the back of his neck. The Death Merchant had come up from behind him!

Zalstoie began to tremble uncontrollably. The low, calm voice behind him only added to his terror.

"Drop the pistol, chubby cheeks, or I'll blow your head off!"

Zalstoie let go of the Makarov with such speed it might have been a red-hot brick. For the first time then, he saw the slim-hipped, broad-shouldered Death Merchant up close. Camellion moved in front of him, picked up the Makarov, and pressed it against Zalstoie's knee, the one that had not been injured.

"Do you know what the knee is composed of, pig farmer?" Camellion asked, staring at the horrified Russian.

"No!"

"There's all sorts of things behind the kneecap. There's the tendon of extensor quadriceps, the patellar tendon, the anterior crucial ligament, and other physical goodies. Just one bullet can turn it all into bloody mush —and that's what's going to happen to both your knees —and your elbows, too—if you don't tell me the truth. Where is Doctor Raya Dubanova?"

Josip Zalstoie's eyes widened. "The traitor Dubanova has been arrested for treason against the state," he choked, his mouth so full of fear-fuzz he could hardly speak. "She is in the headquarters igloo."

"I think you're not telling me the truth," Camellion said with pseudoanger. "I think she and General Vershensky and the rest of the KGB higher-ups are all in the escape-hatch cube." He jabbed the muzzle of the pistol against the Russian's knee. "You'll never walk again, pig farmer!"

"No! No!" screamed Zalstoie, pushing himself against the wall of the building. "I am speaking the truth. Comrade Dubanova is at the headquarters igloo. She is being questioned by General Vershensky and his staff. Only the technicians working in this dome are in the escape cube, but Comrade General Vershensky, h-he ordered the rest of us in Dome 1 to concentrate on you."

"And where are the rest of you KGB bastards?"

Zalstoie's voice quivered with disbelief. "You—you've killed most of them! Only those guarding the headquarters building and the communications cube—they are the only ones left. I swear it! I swear in the name of my dead father and my dead mother that I have told you the truth!"

He imagined the agony he would suffer when the bullet shattered his kneecap. He stared at the Death Merchant, knowing that within the deep blue depths of Camellion's eyes, pure death was grinning at him.

"And I swear in the name of Helel ben-Shahar, Lucifer, Son of the Morning, I'll come back and kill you if you've lied to me!" the Death Merchant said, his left hand moving with such incredible speed that poor Comrade Zalstoie didn't see the blow coming. The edge of Camellion's hand connected with Zalstoie's temple, the perpendicular ax-chop pulling a curtain of blackness over Zalstoie's brain.

The Death Merchant stood erect, looked around him, then began racing at a zigzag angle in the direction of the headquarters igloo. Several minutes later, he paused by the side of the meeting hall and, for some odd reason, thought of a poem by I.K. Chaninsky:

> Znayut vse moyu kvartiru
> Tam zhivu sredi mogil,
> Rvalis tam snaryady zlyie,
> Zhizn svoyu tam polozhil.
> Everybody knows my dwelling;
> There I live among the graves,
> Where the wicked shells were bursting,
> There I lost my youthful life.

Camellion consulted his wristwatch. In fifty-eight minutes, the series of explosions would dissolve Zemlya II into watery oblivion.

Camellion took two hand grenades from the bag on his hip and went to work.

Chapter Ten

Not a single shot was fired at the Death Merchant as he closed in on the communications igloo which was next to the larger cube housing KGB headquarters. Both buildings had windows only in front, and Camellion had no difficulty in moving up along the side of the communications igloo. Gingerly, he looked around the corner, his suspicious eyes sweeping the area.

None of it looked like Central Park. In front of him, 150 feet away, was the curving side of the dome; twelve inches beyond it, the Arctic Ocean. Far to his left was the blasted lock-door of the tube that connected Dome 1 with Dome 2. A score of corpses lay in front of the

129

ripped lock. To Camellion's right another 125 feet was the blown apart lock that separated the dock section, or lock-out chamber, from the rest of Dome 1. And on either side of the lock and above it was the polychrome plastic wall enclosing the giant lock-out chamber, an opaque wall that rose from floor to the curved ceiling of the dome.

I must get inside that radio shack! I must send a message to Albacore. If I don't, I'm as good as dead!

He leaned forward enough to turn and inspect the front of the communications igloo. The door was closed. No doubt they had it braced from the inside. Richard then recalled the windows of the storage cube in Dome 3. Both windows, in the front of the igloo, had been placed there for purely decorative purposes and had been glassless, nothing more than round two-foot holes, because each dome itself, for all practical purposes, was a giant room where the temperature was always a constant seventy-two degrees.

Ah ha! But the front windows of the radio shack igloo were covered over from the inside with metal, in which had been drilled several small holes, each no more than two inches in diameter—proof enough that the KGB gunmen were inside.

Nevertheless, the Death Merchant did have something going for him, in that the small size of the holes made any kind of bilateral vision impossible. The agents inside could only look straight ahead. Good! The meatballs wouldn't be able to detect him as he moved along the front wall.

Richard stepped back to the side of the building. He would need all the speed he could muster. First he took off the two bags, then he slipped the Dragunov music box from his back. Next came four grenades, two of which came from a bag; the last two came from his front pockets. They were the grenades that, five minutes earlier, he had turned into duds by unscrewing their cores and dumping out the main explosive. Now the grenades contained only their primers, which would explode when the pins struck them.

Camellion took the two duds, the two live grenades, and the submachine gun to the corner of the blue igloo, then leaned around and studied the nearest window, six feet away, and the door next to it. Twenty-five feet away, to his left, was the door that opened to the first level of the KGB igloo. Lined up in front of the igloo were six passenger sub-shuttle cars. Two more cars were to the Death Merchant's right, ten feet from the communications shack.

Richard looked again at the window and the door of the radio igloo. Getting inside the building was not a problem. Once inside, his talent for instinctive shooting would have to keep him alive—he hoped. He thought again of AutoMags and wondered how well he could do with them in a close-in fire fight. Now, however, was not the time for idle speculation. He would have to do the job with the weapons he had. If he failed and ended up a corpse, so be it! No one was perfect. Except Jesus Christ! And he'd been lucky. He had a perfect father and had chosen his own mother!

So let's do it! Richard dropped to one knee, pulled a Vitmorkin machine pistol from its hip holster, thumbed off the safety, and laid the weapon on the "ground." Then, as leisurely as if he had been on a target range practicing, he picked up the Dragunov submarine gun and exhausted its magazine with a long burst of fifty 7.62mm slugs, the savage blast dissolving the metal sheet covering the inside of the window, the echo of the intense firing ringing loudly within the dome.

He tossed aside the chatter box, picked up two grenades, pulled the rings and expertly sent them on their way, tossing the dud through the blasted window and rolling the live grenade in front of the door. Then he spun and dove around the corner to the side wall.

The two grenades exploded! The primer of the dud went off with a loud bang, like a big firecracker, a mere whisper compared with the *woom* of the live baby bomb which exploded with a flash of flame and blasted the metal door inward.

The smoke was still clearing when the Death Merchant jumped around the corner and, his eyes on both the door and the window, picked up the last two grenades. He was taking a terrible risk, but he figured that if any KGBs did pop up in the door or try to ice him from the window, he'd still have time to grab the Vitmorkin before the Russians could catch up with their lag time and zero in on him.

Camellion pulled the rings of the two grenades and repeated the process, flinging the dud through the window and rolling the live grenade in front of the now blasted doorway. He snatched up the Vitmorkin and again executed a dive around the corner, opening his mouth and exhaling a loud *ahhhhh* to lessen the pressure of concussion. Camellion rolled over, got to his feet, pulled the other machine pistol from its holster and thumbed off the safety. This was it! Another deep breath, another quick surge of adrenalin, and he had raced around the corner, up the short distance of the wall, and was charging through the smoking doorway, his body at a low profile.

Richard had no way of knowing it, but the odds were on his side. His first blast of submachine guns through the window had killed one agent. The two duds hadn't done any damage—except to demoralize the remaining security personnel—nor had the first grenade that had blown in the metal door. But the second live grenade showered with shrapnel two agents who had stupidly tried to charge through the doorway. The other agents were still alive, expecting a third grenade. They remained down on the floor and crouched behind furniture. The two closest to the wrecked door were dazed from the last thunderous concussion.

The Death Merchant, almost tripping over the two dead agents as he shot through the door, jumped far to the right, toward the bank of short-wave equipment, the Vitmorkin machine pistols roaring. Four KGBs, trying to get up from the floor, died instantly, 9mm slugs chopping pieces of cloth from their blue uniforms before entering their bodies. One agent caught steel death in the side of the jaw. A second got the business in the chest, the impact knocking him back against a table. The third and fourth members of the pig farmer race caught 9mm oblivion in the chest. They had shot for the moon, but had ended up in the Disneyland of the dead. They crashed to the floor like dead trees, one of them falling heavily against a crooked-nosed piece of trash who had managed to pick up his Dragunov submachine gun and was swinging the muzzle toward the Death Merchant. For a moment the man falling against him knocked off his aim, but crooked nose quickly recovered and again jerked the military sight toward Camellion.

Across from crooked nose, toward the rear wall, a sixth KGB louse had jumped up from the floor screaming curses. So mean-looking he could be an instant suspect for the raping of Whistler's mother, he thumbed his Stechkin to full automatic, spot-sighted on Camellion, and pulled the trigger.

The Death Merchant, who had spotted him as well as crooked nose, dodged to the right, the Vitmorkins in his hands snarling as he made a dive in the direction of the back wall. The short burst from the Stechkin missed him by several feet, but the sweeping longer burst from the submachine gun almost zinged him into Dead Man's City.

Camellion yelled in pain when a slug burned across his left rib cage, its red-hot passage raising a long mark that quickly bloated with blood; a second 7.62mm piece of steel tore through his pants and ice-picked across his hip, bringing with it a burning stab of pain. The third slug cut across the top of his skull, so close to the bone it parted his hair.

But he had not missed the two security agents. The Russian with the Stechkin had received a slug in the midsection and one in the chest. He lay dying on the floor, face-down in a pool of blood, not far from the Commie creep who had tried to blow up Camellion with the Dragunov submachine gun.

Moving quickly to one side, Camellion directed his attention at the last two Russians, the two agents down by the doorway, who had recovered sufficiently from concussion to get into the action. Not that it did them any good. Instead of being jet commuters, they were bus riders whose time had come to take up residence in eternity.

Lev Stovbun fired his Red Army Tokarev pistol, the big weapon booming like a Colt .45, while Cyril Kommukin snapped off a shot with a 9mm Makarov automatic. Both shots sounded almost as one as Richard ducked to one side, dropped almost to the floor, and jerked to the right at the same time that the two Russians again fired and again missed because of Camellion's lightning-quick movements.

Camellion chuckled. "Turn out the red lights in your mothers' bedrooms, pig farmers," he sneered as he fired four times in rapid succession. One 9mm missed Kommukin by half an inch; it went bye-bye through the open door. The second pretty little piece of steel stabbed Kommukin just below the hollow of the throat, punctured his innominate artery, and bored out at an angle through the right side of his back. Belching great gobs of blood, he looked horrified, dropped, and proceeded to die, unaware that Stovbun would join him within a second or two.

Stovbun caught the last two 9mm bullets from Camellion, both popping him in the forehead, the violent impact scattering flesh, bone, blood, and brains for several feet. Stovbun's arms flew up. He twisted to one side, fell, and lay still.

The battle was over. The Death Merchant stood up, shoved fresh clips into the machine pistols, and went over to the radio banks on the other side of the room. He didn't gasp at what he saw, nor did his heart skip any beats; he was too accustomed and too hardened to the unexpected for such useless emotion.

No use to kid himself. He would never send a message to *Albacore* on any of these sets. While the 15-80 meters receiver and the MHz and kHz receivers were unmarked, the blast of 7.62 slugs from one agent's Dragunov submachine gun had reduced the transmitters to useless junk.

Camellion tried the brass-pounder's oscillator key— dead!

He had the feeling that he would soon be dead, too.

Chapter Eleven

The most despondent man in Zemlya II was General Rostislav Pavlovich Vershensky. He would have to bear the full responsibility for what the Death Merchant had done, and was doing, to Zemlya II. It was General Vershensky who would have to answer to the center in Moscow. If he lived to get to Moscow! General Vershensky's three aides and the regular agents with them in the file section were just as miserable, every man realizing what the terrible Death Merchant was trying to do—he was trying to rescue Comrad Doctor Raya Dubanova. And even General Vershensky had to admit, grudgingly, that within a very short time Camellion had done a lot to achieve that goal. Not only had the Death Merchant escaped from the storage igloo in Dome 3, but he had also blasted his way through the locks into the control dome and had annihilated the security forces that had tried to stop him.

To make matters more perilous for the Russians, the control dome was cut off from the rest of the base except Domes 2 and 3, both of which were of no consequence. The Death Merchant had slaughtered all the KGB agents in Dome 2. And Dome 3 was only a storage dome.

The designers of Zemlya II had not considered the possibility of a dangerous enemy agent running amok in the undersea city and blasting the tube locks with rocket shells. When Camellion had destroyed the locks with rocket shells, he had damaged the relays of the automatic control system to the extent that the locks could not be reopened from the main control center in the KGB headquarters igloo. This meant that the KGB agents and other personnel in Domes 4 and 5 could not enter Dome 3. They couldn't even use explosives to blast the locks. The charges were in the armory in Dome 2.

After Camellion had eliminated the guards around the lock opening to the control dome, a raging General Vershensky had deployed his remaining agents within the communications center and the headquarters igloo, ignoring the pleas of Colonel Pyotr Wrangel that he send half a dozen men to the armory in Dome 2 to get hand grenades and a heavy machine gun.

"Comrade General Vershensky, as long as we are without grenades, the Death Merchant has a great advantage," Colonel Wrangel pointed out, for once disagreeing with Vershensky.

General Vershensky remained adamant in his refusal, stressing the lack of men. "We have less than thirty-five men in this igloo and in the communications center," he said in a band-saw voice. "We can't risk sending men outside these two buildings and risk losing them to Camellion. Nor is there time to send any men on such a dangerous errand. Already that murderous CIA assassin is killing those useless idiots by the air compressors. He would no doubt murder any men we tried to send through the tube to Dome II. No! I will send no one. All the men will stay within this building and inside the communications center."

Colonel Wrangel, Major Sedin, and Captain Tur did not argue with General Vershensky. What was the use? He had made up his mind. Nonetheless, all three men were convinced that Comrade Vershensky was making a serious mistake. Captain Tur thought that Vershensky was indulging in a hasty generalization about the Death Merchant. Even if the Death Merchant did succeed in shooting his way past the agents at the air compressors, it did not follow that he would invariably kill any agents sent to Dome 2. He might not even see them. If he did, there was a good chance he wouldn't be able to reach them. That Vershensky with his peasant mentality. How could such a simpleton have risen to the rank of general?

Captain Tur thought of how completely Dome 1 was isolated from the four other domes. Even telephone communications had been knocked out by Camellion's blasting of the locks.

Sitting there, his eyes watching the various television monitoring screens, Tur told himself how he would handle the situation had he been in command. Since the Death Merchant Comrade wanted Raya Dubanova so badly, why not use the slut as bait?

That is exactly the strategy General Vershensky put into operation when one of the TV monitor cameras picked up the Death Merchant running toward the communications igloo and his image appeared briefly on the screen.

General Vershensky got to his feet, glared at Raya and growled, "Come, we will go to the second level and wait for the Death Merchant in the file room. If that murderous maniac succeeds in getting past the men in the control room, he will never be able to get into the upstairs file room." He walked over to Raya Dubanova and slapped her hard across the face. "And if he does, you damned traitorous bitch, he will have to kill you first to get to us!"

Minutes later, Wrangel, Sedin, and Tur saw what Vershensky meant after they were in the second level file room and Vershensky was giving orders to the ten KGB agents in the big room.

"Move those filing cabinets out from the wall," he commanded, "and place them in a square ten feet from the door. They'll make excellent protection."

Vershensky turned to Major Ivan Sedin, who was holding a disconsolate Raya Dubanova tightly by her arm.

"Put the bitch in a chair five feet in front of the door," the general said in a harsh voice. "If Camellion does get this far, we'll have the traitor between him and us. We'll kill the capitalist assassin the second he comes through the door."

Captain Tur placed a chair five feet from the doorway, which lacked a door (doors were not considered necessary inside the KGB headquarters building), and Major Sedin forced Raya Dubanova to sit down, shoving her roughly onto the chair.

"Comrade General, there is the possibility that the

Death Merchant will use hand grenades," offered Colonel Wrangel. "He is not a man to take unnecessary chances."

General Vershensky, watching Major Sedin force Raya Dubanova's arms through the slats in the back of the chair and them snap handcuffs around her wrists, rubbed his hands together, as if enjoying himself.

"The filing cases are crammed with files," he said confidently. "They will absorb shrapnel and concussion. We will be behind them. As for that bitch"—he pointed at Raya Dubanova—"she deserves anything she gets."

Richard Camellion, flattened against a wall of the KGB headquarters building, recognized one all-important fact: if he could get Raya Dubanova safely away from the KGB, and he and Raya Dubanova could reach one of the "passenger little-boats" in the lock-out section of the dome and escape to the Arctic Ocean, they might survive. Survive? How long? How long before they were picked up by Russian navy patrol boats? Or froze to death? Yet it was the only chance he had. So why not dream the impossible, conceive the inconceivable, and try to make possible the impossible. Why not? He had nothing to lose but his life. All people died, some sooner than others. It was only a question of when.

But first things first. *How would I handle the situation if I were General Vershenshy? He's a very cautious pig farmer, and won't leave anything to chance.*

Camellion began working on the premise that Vershensky and his aides and what was left of the KGB was waiting for him in the headquarters igloo. Waiting, yes. But where? Where would Vershensky and his corn-pone meatballs be holding Raya Dubanova?

Richard had carefully memorized the interior of the KGB headquarters cube when Captain Yubishkanonavitch and his guards had first taken him before General Vershensky, and now he recalled the floor plan, remembering every detail he had seen.

The outside door had opened to the main control room. Yubishkanonavitch and the five nitwits had marched him across one end of the control room to General Vershensky's office, Camellion had seen a doorway, and filing cabinets beyond the doorway. Okay, so there was a file room next to Vershensky's office.

Half of the headquarters building had a second level built over Vershensky's office and the file room next to the office. This second story was reached by means of steps which were on the same side of the control room as the office and the file room. The Death Merchant had even counted the steps—eleven of them that terminated at a rectangular landing nine feet above the floor of the control room. On the landing was a doorway that led into a room.

The Death Merchant's face, dirty from the smoke of exploded shells, became very grim. *Yes, Vershensky and his boys will wait in that room at the top of the stairs. There's not a better defense spot in the entire building.*

Raya Dubanova? *Vershensky and his KGB bastards will have her in such a position that I'll have to kill every one in the room to get to her!*

It all added up to a theoretical impossibility. *Gerald Ford has more chance of being elected President of the United States than I have of rescuing Doctor Dubanova.*

Camellion looked around the corner of the building. The front was almost thirty feet long. In the center of the wall was a door. On each side of it were two windows, each covered with sheet metal.

Thinking that he was probably going to his own execution, Richard began creeping toward the door, hunched so far down that no one would be able to see him through peepholes when he passed beneath the first two windows. He arrived at the door, placed two hand grenades in front of the door, and crawled back to the corner of the building. He went around to the side of the building, flattened himself against the wall, and aimed a Vitmorkin machine pistol around the corner, judging the distance and angle as he pointed the barrel downward. He pulled the trigger; the machine pistol, on full automatic, roared, and the two hand grenades exploded, the big blasts tearing off the locked door and flinging it backward into the control room, the terrific concussion pounding on Camellion's ear drums.

Very quickly he put a fresh magazine into the Vitmorkin, shoved the machine pistol back into its holster, picked up the Dragunov submachine gun, and charged around the corner, triggering off short but deadly bursts at both the first two windows and the smoking doorway. Only an idiot would have tried to step through the doorway or attempt to remove the coverings over the windows.

Camellion stopped a few feet to one side of the doorway, fired another short burst sideways through the opening, then dropped the submachine gun and at the same time pulled a Vitmorkin. Just as frantically he reached into one bag, took out a hand grenade, and pulled its ring by looping it over the small buckle on a strap over his chest, then jerking the grenade forward. He tossed it around the short corner through the doorway. He had already taken out the second grenade and was pulling its ring when the first grenade detonated. Richard tossed the second grenade through the doorway into the control room, throwing it so that it would roll toward the far end of the room.

Four more grenades followed in quick succession, the crashing concussions tearing at the Death Merchant and making the front wall shake violently; and with the roar of the detonations came screams of agony, the loud rending and tearing of metal, and the crashing of various pieces of equipment as the explosions pitched them across the room.

The Death Merchant returned the machine pistol to its holster, picked up the Dragunov machine gun, took a deep breath, and charged in low through the doorway, straight into the hell of the control room. To one side of his mind he was aware that something had changed within Dome 1, but he was far too busy to dwell on the puzzle. He didn't realize it at the time that almost half of the lights on the ceiling of the dome had flickered out.

The six grenades, spaced out by Camellion, had done their destructive work well. Control banks had been blasted into broken knobs, twisted wires, torn cables, shattered dials, and levers and switches that had been torn loose from their foundations. Electric fires burned in two of the panels, the blue flames making a sound like corn beginning to pop.

Within the Dome itself, the giant fan, lacking power from the control center, had stopped blowing on the giromill, whose vertical blades no longer moved. The smoke detection and air purification station was also dead, its power from the control room having been cut by one of Camellion's grenades. However, the air compressors were still in operation, their piston arms *woom-woom-wooming* up and down methodically like monstrous triphammers. The air compressors, on automatic relays that had switched them over to other control center for twenty-six minutes, after which they would either have to be switched to the main power unit or die.

The control room itself was wrecked, stinking of burning rubber and melted wire and plastic, while layers of smoke drifted like long blue gray shrouds over the seven mangled bodies of the KGB agents killed by the grenades. The five security men still alive—one of whom was Captain Paul Yubishkanonavitch—were so dazed and mentally disorganized they had difficulty deciding whether they were alive, were dead, or were dying! Concussion had rendered them so deaf that they wouldn't have been able to hear the end of the world had it occurred!

On the other hand, there wasn't anything wrong with the eyesight of the five agents. The only catch was that by the time they spotted the figure of Camellion, who was ducking and dodging all over the place, they were also staring into naked death, into the flashing muzzle of his submachine gun.

To the left of Camellion, Lieutenant Leo Nyghzev was trying to swing his Simonov automatic rifle toward Camellion when a couple of 7.62mm slugs tore away his face and kicked his brains out the back of his skull. He fell backward as though hit by a cannonball.

Basil Zdebskis, six feet behind Nyghzev, was the next pig farmer to get burned out of life and existence by a line of Dragunov steel that almost cut him in half as it chopped him across the stomach. He snorted, doubled over, and fell forward, hitting the floor like he was about to do a somersault.

Camellion dodged to the right just in time to avoid a chain of fire from Mikhail Ogborg, who had triggered off a stream of 7.62 AK steel at him. The blast skimmed by the Death Merchant, burning the air six inches to his left and cutting through the doorway in the front wall.

Richard fired the Dragunov as he hit the floor on his hip, moving the submachine gun in a semicircle, jerking the hot muzzle from Ogborg to Aleksei Sakhariv and Paul Yubishkanonavitch, the last two Russians—ten feet to the right of Ogborg—as close together as easy money and bad conscience.

Camellion's submachine gun hosed out steel death. Six big 7.62mm slugs ripped across Ogborg's chest, ripped him wide open, and kicked him into hell with both eyes closed and his bloody mouth wide open.

Aleksei Sakhariv was the next pig farmer to get cut apart by Camellion's stream of metal death, finding in his dying that it's only a blink in time between the bright light of life and the bitter darkness of death. Sakhariv's body was punched full of holes, and he died in the middle of taking a deep breath, a hundredth of a second before Captain Paul Yubishkanonavitch's luck went all bad—and from the expression of pure horror on Yubishkanonavitch's face, just before the bullets bit into his body, he knew it. Then suddenly he knew only blackness. Two 7.62mms broke his skull open and scattered his brain like an egg thrown against a brick wall. At the same instant, hot slugs chastised his chest, stomach and groin. Eyes wide open, Yubishkanonavitch toppled, his cut-up corpse looking like it had been run over twice by the 6:45 Special.

Ever since Raya Dubanova had regained consciousness, she had pretended to be more hurt and dazed than she actually was. Once she had been taken into custody, she automatically assumed that she and Camellion and every human being in Zemlya II would die when the final second clicked from the timers and the nitrostarch detonated.

In spite of Doctor Dubanova's acceptance of what she considered the inevitable, she did not intend to let the Death Merchant walk into the carefully prepared trap in the second level file room. With her hands manacled through the back of the chair, she sat only five feet from the doorway, black filing cabinets surrounding her on the other three sides, the evil-looking muzzles of automatic weapons poking through the five-inch space between each case.

Raya had closed her eyes and had prayed during the grenade barrage in the control room, the pounding concussions rattling even her teeth. A few minutes later, with the doomful echoes dashing back and forth in her brain, she heard the ferocious firing of automatic weapons and, above the typewriterlike roaring, the furious voice of Comrade General Vershensky, "Get ready, comrades! the Death Merchant is attacking downstairs!"

Raya Dubanova knew what she had to do, the only possible thing she could do. She jumped up, her sudden movement awkward and restraining because of the chair she had to take with her. Moving as quickly as she could, carrying the chair on her backside, she half-hobbled, half-stumbled to the doorway, expecting at any moment she would feel the agony of slugs cutting into her flesh.

None came! General Vershensky and his men had been caught completely off guard, Doctor Dubanova's unexpected movement leaving them thunderstruck and too surprised to do anything but gape. And by the time Vershensky and his men recovered from their astonishment, she had moved through the doorway and was trying to get down the steps, well out of their line of sight.

"Get her!" screamed Vershensky, consumed with such a rage that his fleshy face turned almost purple. "Kill that traitorous bitch! She's responsible for all this trouble!"

His chest rising and falling with labored breathing, the Death Merchant got to his feet, his right hip throbbing with pain, the right side of his pants sticky with wetness. The wound, caused by the bullet that had

143

grazed his hip in the radio shack, was not serious, but landing on his hip had caused it to throb again.

He dropped to one knee when, in a flash, he saw a figure on the landing at the top of the stairs, a familiar figure which made him hold his fire. Seeing him, Doctor Dubanova yelled as she stumbled slowly down the steps —"The doorway at the top, Camellion. There are—"

Her words were drowned out in the staccato roaring of Richard's submachine gun. The stream of hot steel cut upward through the railing around the landing and stabbed into the chest of Dmitrevich Higalin, the KGB agent who had reached the doorway first. Two more 7.62mm Dragunov bullets punched the side of Emil Borodine, who was right behind Higalin. Borodine cried out in pain and fell back into the file room while Higalin fell dead on the metal landing, his legs still inside the doorway.

Doctor Dubanova came down the stairs as fast as she could, her plain-featured face a mask of fear and anxiety. She was hunched over until her body was almost bent double, her head at a level with her knees, this position necessary in order that the legs of the chair could clear the steps behind her.

"To the door! Get to the outside door!" Richard shouted to Dr. Dubanova, who had reached the last step. "I'll cover you!"

He sent another burst of submachine gun slugs through the doorway at the top of the stairs. Hearing the overworked weapon click on empty, he slung it over one shoulder and pulled both Vitmorkin machine pistols. He was almost too late!

Two more Russkies appeared in the upper doorway, one armed with an AK-47 assault rifle, the second pig farmer carrying a Stechkin machine pistol with an extra-long thirty-four-cartridge magazine. He was trying to aim down at Raya Dubanova who was halfway to the outside door.

"Eat lead, you Slavic saps!" Richard said, then raised both machine pistols and fired instinctively, the big pistols roaring and jumping in his hands. The two nincompoops also jumped—straight into the final oblivion.

A big bad bullet caught the Russkie with the Stechkin

144

underneath the chin, the hot piece of copper-coated steel cutting upward through his mouth, digging a tunnel through his brain, and blowing off the top of his head—hair and bone flying all the way to the high ceiling.

Two more pellets of 9mm steel hit the Russian with the AK-47 and lifted him a few inches off the floor. One slug sliced upward through his spleen and left lung; the second bullet knifed him just below the navel, giving him the final bellyache of his life. Crying out "Uh, Uh, Uh," he pitched backward toward the doorway. The other agent nose-dived down the stairs, his Stechkin clanging loudly alongside him.

"Come on down, you backward pig farmers!" the Death Merchant yelled in Russian. "I have lots of presents for you. Come on, Vershensky, you fat dummy!"

He fired four more shots through the doorway on the landing at the top of the stairs. At the same time, he began backing out of the control room, following Dr. Dubanova, who reached the doorway as he fired the fifth, sixth, and seventh shots.

Once she reached the outside of the building, Dr. Dubanova waited to one side of the door. Camellion, however, didn't even glance in her direction. Instead, he holstered the two Vitmorkin machine pistols, took a hand grenade from the carrier bag, pulled the ring, and flipped the grenade through the doorway, tossing it toward the stairs.

Four seconds later the grenade went off with a roar, followed by a short scream of agony and the *plink-plink-plinking* of shrapnel hitting metal.

There were more shouts from inside the control room Camellion recognized Major Sedin's frantic voice—"Get back! The son of a bitch is using grenades!"

Within the next few minutes, Camellion tossed in five more grenades, spacing them out, both in time and in directions. A warm, satisfied feeling floated through his body as the grenades exploded and destroyed more of the interior of the control room.

Camellion, confident that it would be at least five minutes, if not longer, before Vershensky and his boys could get up enough courage to charge across the control room, turned his attention to Raya Dubanova. It was

145

then that he noticed the strange, abnormal silence in the dome, and saw that four of the overhead sodium-vapor lights were flickering on and off like blue-white advertising signs; and for the first time he noticed Doctor Dubanova's battered face, her swollen jaw, black eye, and puffed lips. General Vershensky and his fellow sadists had not been very gentle with Doctor Dubanova.

"The air compressors have stopped, and the lights are about to go out," Raya Dubanova whispered hoarsely, staring at Camellion. She paused, then added, "Death Merchant, you have turned Zemlya II into a graveyard of the doomed!"

Richard noted the subtle resentment and the hint of accusation in her tired voice. He knew the reason: although she had made contact with the CIA and was willing to reveal extremely vital information to "the Company," the Russians in Zemlya II were still her people. Why then had she betrayed her countrymen by contacting the CIA? Whatever she knew, whatever her secret might be, it was more important than even loyalty!

"Turn around, *Babushka*," Camellion said as he pulled out a machine pistol, "and I'll part those handcuffs."

"I'm not your grandmother, Camellion!" snapped Dr. Dubanova, turning her back to the Death Merchant. "I'm not anyone's grandmother, and I'm glad I'm not. The grandmothers I know are only grandmothers of selfishness."

"Pull against the chain with your wrists," Camellion ordered. "I want the chain as taut as possible."

When the links between the handcuffs were rigid, Richard put the muzzle of the machine pistol against the middle link, pulled the trigger, and the slug parted the chain, freeing Dr. Dubanova's wrists from the back of the chair. The chair fell and she began rubbing her pained arms, the chains on the handcuffs clinking from each wrist.

Camellion ran back to the side of the doorway, pulled out his last grenade, jerked the ring, and flipped the grenade around the metal frame into the smoking control room. He grinned when he heard it explode, hoping that he had killed General Vershensky, and thinking of how the CIA never used such words as "kill" or "assassinate." Field agents and top-level executives alike preferred to use such terms as "eliminate," "terminate," "remove from the scene," "retire," and "alter the health" of various "targets." But to say "kill"—never!

The Death Merchant chuckled—That's what I am doing. I'm "altering the health of targets!"

He went back to Dr. Dubanova, who was flexing her numb arms.

"We've got to get to one of the "little-boats" in the dock lock-out chamber," he said, nodding toward the six sub-shuttle cars parked in front of the KGB headquarters building. "We'll use a sub-shuttle car. I'll drive —come on!"

They hurried to the first sub-shuttle car in line and got in the front seat, Camellion sliding behind the small wheel. Within seconds the vehicle was operational and he had it humming toward the demolished lock-door of the dock lock-out chamber, swerving the car widely and wildly to avoid the rain of slugs from General Vershensky and his men, who were firing as they ran from the headquarters building to a sub-shuttle car to follow in pursuit.

As Richard guided the car through the blown apart lock-door, the last light on the ceiling flickered out, and the igloo section of the dome was plunged into darkness. Nonetheless, the sodium-vapor lights in the dock section, deriving their power from a generator independent of the control room in the KGB building, burned with a steady blue white glow.

The dock section of the l.o.c. was deserted, and if there were any KGB security personnel around, the Death Merchant and Raya Dubanova did not see them. They couldn't help but notice that the mooring section was shaped like an inverted right angle, with the top, twice the length of the side, filled with long docks on either side of slips large enough to accommodate even nuclear submarine; and that is exactly what was in the last slip—a sleek dark gray U-boat of the 9,000-ton Delta class!

The short section of the inverted right angle contained

smaller slips, some of which were empty, others filled with "passenger little-boats," looking like baby whales that were three-fourths submerged—six of the little subs to be exact.

"We'll take a little sub that has an l.o.c.," Camellion said, glancing furiously at the Russian nuclear sub. "I hope you can tell which sub has an l.o.c. and which hasn't."

"Those with a lock-out chamber have their entry hatches in the center of the hull, like a conventional submarine," Dr. Dubanova replied. She looked sadly and fearfully at the nuclear sub. "What does it matter. How can we fight that monster over there? It can easily outrun us and send men to board us. And General Vershensky will follow in a 'little-boat.'"

The big nuclear submarine, several hundred feet to the right and a hundred feet ahead of Camellion and Dubanova, was about to get under way. On the bow, sailors were casting off lines and responding to orders being shouted by officers on the bridge deck of the tall sail, or conning tower. Both the sailors and the officers ducked for cover when they saw the sub-shuttle car roll to the "little-boat" mooring section of the docks and the Death Merchant bring it to a halt on the concrete parkway. Then they saw the two figures jump from the vehicle and run toward the steps that would take them down to the slips where the baby subs were moored. Within a few moments the two figures were moving down the steps, and the Russians on the nuclear sub could no longer see them.

"If the nuclear submarine doesn't sink us with torpedoes and we can somehow escape General Vershensky, it is possible we might survive," Raya Dubanova said, her breath coming in great gasps from the effort of her exertion as she huffed and puffed along the dock.

"Yeah, and if a hen ate tacks she could lay a carpet," Camellion responded, privately estimating their chances for life at just about zero. But at least the under-the-ocean city would be destroyed. *Some consolation! But who knows?*

Dr. Dubanova led Camellion to the second baby sub

resting within a few feet of the side of the metal dock, and they soon reached the top center hatch by climbing the metal rungs welded to the rounded hull.

"I don't know if they can be of any help, but there are deep-diving suits and explosive mines on board this kind of submersible, the kind with a lock-out chamber," the Russian woman said, watching Camellion spin the lock-wheel. "We use these vessels for construction purposes. Divers blast rock and other underwater obstacles with the mines."

Lifting the three-foot hatch cover, Richard jerked his head toward Dr. Dubanova, his eyes glowing with surprise and interest.

"Get in," he ordered and glanced upward toward the parkway, ignoring Raya Dubanova, who swung her legs over the rim of the hatch and started to climb down the ladder.

The Death Merchant's face became sinister. Another sub-shuttle car had moved through the lock-door. Ah . . . Comrade General Rostislav Pavlovich and what was left of his men had arrived.

Richard crawled into the hatch and, standing on the ladder, closed the cover and began spinning the inside lock-wheel—all to the litany of the first submachine gun slugs, which ricocheted hollowly off the outside hull of the U-boat.

Camellion slid down the short ladder and joined Raya Dubanova, who had turned on the lights and was motioning to him to follow her. Hunched over to keep from bumping his head on metal pipes, Richard moved along behind the Russian scientist.

"Those mines, you mentioned," Camellion said. "Are they magnetic? And where are the deep-diving suits and the l.o.c. aboard this tub?"

"Yes, all the mines are magnetic," Dr. Dubanova answered. "That is because they are used also to remove underwater obstructions made of metal, such as sunken ships and what have you. As you will recall, a lot of Allied shipping was sunk in this area during World War II."

She stopped within the narrow, dimly lighted confines of the passageway, turned to him, and tapped on the side of a bulkhead type door. "Here, in this compartment are diving suits, mines, and electric prods for protection against vicious marine life. The compartment next to this one—the door is on the inside—is the lock-out chamber. It's of the dry type, and there is no hatch cover over the drop-out chute."

Eight feet forward was another oval door. Dr. Dubanova pulled back on the vertical lever; the door swung open, and she stepped into the control compartment. The Death Merchant followed, watching with interest as she settled her heavy body into the bucket seat in front of the curved control board. The first thing she did was switch on the air circulation and purification system, then the television cameras, whose screens, over the control panel, revealed the entire area around the submarine. Now all that was visible was dark water.

"Doctor, how fast can you get this boat through the diving tube and out into the Arctic Ocean?" Camellion asked, furrows of intense thought forming on his forehead.

"Do you have a plan, Mr. Camellion?" Dr. Dubanova flipped a switch marked *l.o.c. pressure*. She then pushed a large red button above that bore the label *power*. At once, a low humming began flowing through the vessel.

The Death Merchant answered: "Once we're away from Zemlya II, I'll go out through the l.o.c. and plant a few mines against General Vershensky's boat, if he follows. And with any kind of luck, I might be able to sink that big nuclear baby before any of our 'friends' can do anything about it. Come to think of it, there's something you should know. I couldn't make contact with *Albacore*. A KGB boy machine-gunned the radio sets. We're strictly on our own."

Dr. Dubanova turned in the bucket seat and stared up at him, her small eyes blinking in disbelief. "What you have in mind is certain death! Sheer madness!"

"What I have in mind is living, life for both of us, at least for a while," Camellion said. He jerked up his right wrist and looked at his wrist watch. "But you'll have to move this steel coffin damn fast. In twenty-eight minutes, Zemlya II will be blown off the face of the earth. Correction, off the bottom of the sea."

"Within the next five minutes," Dr. Dubanova said, swiveling around in the bucket seat to face the control board. "Within five minutes I'll have us outside the dome and the air pressure in the diving lock will be sufficient for you to leave the vessel."

She pulled the lever that would allow water to pour into the submergence tanks, and she surprised Camellion by saying, "From the way you act, you must have been born under the astrological sign of Scorpio. Like most Scorpios, you insist on attempting the impossible, on defying death even at the final moment."

Camellion smiled. How about that! Not only did Dr. Dubanova believe in the Christian type of sadistic hellfire god, but apparently she believed in the nonsense of astrology.

"Sorry, Doctor, but I don't believe in the magic of astrology," Camellion said, chuckling mildly. "Anyhow, I'm not a Scorpio. I'm Sagittarius and we're notoriously hard to convince!" Again he laughed. "To me, astrology is nothing more than the nonsense of 'magic,' which would have us believe it knows the secrets of the universe."

"Nyet, you are mistaken," Dr. Dubanova replied. "Astrology does not offer an explanation of the laws of the universe, nor why the universe exists. What it does is to show us that there is a correspondence between macrocosm and microcosm—that there is a rhythm to the universe, and that man's own life partakes of this rhythm. That, Mr. Camellion, is the secret of astrology."

"Uh huh. Well, speaking of secrets, what's yours, Doctor, the one so important that it forced you to contact American intelligence? Since you're convinced that we'll soon be standing before the bar of God, what harm is there in telling me?"

The submarine submerged, and Camellion became aware that the boat was moving, the humming growing louder as Dr. Dubanova fed more electric power to the engines.

"The world is going to end," Dr. Dubanova said in an odd voice. "I don't mean the planet itself. I mean world civilization. Within the next fifteen years, the planet will convulse, the oceans will roll over every continent, and all civilization will be destroyed. We have scientific evidence that this will occur, but now is not the time to discuss it, nor why I—why we—chose to inform your government."

Amazed, Richard left the control compartment and moved toward the chamber containing the diving suits, the magnetic mines, and the electric fish prods.

Civilization will be destroyed, she said. If it did happen, the Death Merchant thought, it might be a good thing. Perhaps a new era was needed. No one could deny that man's present civilization wasn't worth a damn. There was no justice in the democracy of the West, and even less honesty in the Communism of the East. Man did have his religion to console him! Yeah, the consolation of myth, madness, and moral imbecility. In the West, "religious" people would sleep through the Sermon on the Mount, if a buck was involved. The East wasn't any better.

A smile flowed over the Death Merchant's mouth. Maybe the world would end in fifteen years, but right now he had work to do. If he failed, his world would end that very same day.

Chapter Twelve

Major Sedin, who was watching the television screens above the control board, turned the guide wheel controlling the rudder and pressed down on the left foot pedal which controlled the hydroplanes. General Vershensky, sitting next to Sedin, felt his body pushed back into the bucket seat as the bow of the small U-boat moved upward and to the right.

Colonel Pyotr Wrangel and Captain Vasily Tur, standing behind Sedin and Vershensky, braced themselves by holding onto hand-holds on the side walls of the compartment. All four men men kept their eyes glued to the five television screens, and suddenly, in the bow screen, there it was: the dark silhouette of another "passenger little-boat."

"There they are! Vershensky shouted, his eyes glittering in triumph. "How far do you estimate the distance, Comrade Major?"

Major Sedin studied the screen for a moment. "Not more than ten meters, perhaps a little more or a little less. I have no doubt we can catch up with them." Sedin pulled the power lever out another notch, and the humming within the boat grew louder.

General Vershensky remained silent, his thoughts a raging maelstrom of frustration, a whirlpool of ignominious defeat over how the Death Merchant had wrecked Zemlya II. A realist, Vershensky was not a man to rationalize; he knew Zemlya II was doomed. With the air compressors not functioning, it was only a matter of time before the ocean crushed the five domes. Much worse, the damned Death Merchant had wrecked Vershensky's career in the KGB, for he knew there was no excuse he could give the center, no explanation as to why he, as commander of the KGB force at Zemlya II, had failed to stop a single individual from annihilating almost half the security guards at the underseas base. Vershensky admitted another fact of life within the KGB—there always had to be a fall guy. And he would be it. By the time the center got finished with him, he'd be lucky if he didn't spend the rest of his life in a gulag!

"What puzzles me is why they're going so slow," Colonel Wrangel said, "unless something is wrong with their boat. They seem to be slowing more and more."

Captain Tur cleared his throat. "Do you suppose that the traitor Dubanova and the Death Merchant have some kind of plan for destroying us or the nuclear sub?"

Along with the other three men, he continued to watch the "little-boat" ahead moving very slowly away from Zemlya II, its depth not more than 250 feet below the surface of the Arctic Ocean.

Major Sedin said, "We can't see the nuclear submarine, and since it is beyond the vision of our cameras,

Comrade Dubanova and the Death Merchant can't see it either.

"But surely Commander Linsoklitisch would not leave the area?" Captain Tur said. "He would not do that; I am sure."

"No, he would not," Vershensky said crossly, "but you should know that Comrade Linsoklitisch is not going to risk a valuable nuclear submarine to put out a fire which has already burned the chestnuts to a crisp. He is aware that Zemlya II is on the edge of a grave. And he has no way of knowing what the Death Merchant might do. How does he know that the crazy *Amerikanski* isn't willing to blow himself up and try to take the nuclear sub with him?"

Or us! thought Captain Tur. No one could argue against the incredible courage of the Death Merchant. He was capable of anything! Tur still found it impossible to believe that Camellion had single-handedly attacked first the communications center then the headquarters cube. The damage the Death Merchant had done! Only five KGB regulars had survived in the headquarters igloo, and one man had been so badly wounded by the Death Merchant's last grenade that they had been forced to leave him behind. By now he had probably bled to death. The four KGB regulars who remained alive were suiting up in the compartment next to the lock-out chamber. It was General Vershensky's plan to send the four outside to catch up with the other submarine and plant magnetic mines against its hull.

Captain Tur felt a chill crawl along his backbone. Why couldn't the Death Merchant have the same plan? Why couldn't the Death Merchant leave his boat, swim over to the KGB sub, and slap mines against its sides?

Captain Tur knew that General Vershensky was thinking along the same lines when he saw Vershensky turn around in his seat and look at Colonel Wrangel, and heard him say, "Comrade Colonel, the security and the operation of the construction 'little-boats' were your responsibility and in your department. Tell me, did every 'little-boat' used on construction projects carry explosives?"

"The Death Merchant could blow us out of the water,"

Colonel Wrangel said, anticipating what Vershensky was thinking. "There are mines and diving suits aboard his boat. I am positive because only a few days ago I went over the latest operation reports of the 'little-boats,' and none had been on any construction project."

General Vershensky peered speculatively at Colonel Wrangel.

"Comrade Wrangel, I want you to go along with our men when we catch up with the Death Merchant's boat and they attach the mines to the side of his submarine. Our men will need all the help they can get. Wounded jackals always turn and fight when cornered."

Colonel Wrangel, turning pale and fumbling nervously with the flap of his holster, regarded swimming over to Camellion's sub in the same light that the Pope of Rome considered suicide.

Before Wrangel could speak, General Vershensky snapped, "Don't stand there like a statue, Comrade. Get going."

Without a word, Colonel Wrangel left the control compartment and closed the bulkhead door.

"Look, Comrades! The Death Merchant's submarine has stopped!" Major Sedin exclaimed, his nervous voice charged with excitement. "I think they've stopped deliberately. It can't be the boat, or it would be going to the sea floor."

Sedin, Captain Tur, and General Vershensky stared at the television screen. The submarine ahead had indeed stopped. It hung poised in the water, its port side facing the bow of the KGB boat. To all appearances it was dead in the water.

Vershensky laid a hand on Major Sedin's arm. "Stop the boat, Comrade. It might be some kind of trick on the Death Merchant's part. Let's see what he does before we close in."

The three Russians waited, each man staring at the submarine, each man secretly afraid.

Chapter Thirteen

Throughout the world, there are two basic kinds of lock-out chambers, the "wet" and the "dry." The most common kind is the wet chamber, in which a diver enters a compartment and floods it with water. When the chamber is completely flooded, and the pressure inside is equal to the pressure of the surrounding ocean, the driver opens the hatch and swims out.

The dry lock-out chamber, in which air pressure inside the lock prevents water from pouring in the open diving well, is not common and is used primarily in experimental underwater installations. Such dry chambers are never used in submarines. For this reason, the Death Merchant, standing in the l.o.c., had to admire the marine technology of the Soviet Union. You had to give the pig farmers credit. A dry lock-out system on a midget sub was quite an achievement.

Checking his suit, Camellion also had to admire the Russian-designed deep-diving life-support system. It was every bit as good as anything the United States Navy had. The suit was of the closed-circuit type, the exotic breathing mixture of oxygen and helium, with just a touch of neon, being continuously recycled by the electrolyte cryogenic system which provided carbon dioxide and humidity control by freezing these constituents out of the atmosphere breathed by the diver. The fresh air was then returned to the twin tanks on the diver's back. Such a closed system did not leave a trail of air bubbles. Another advantage to breathing an exotic mixture was that it eliminated the danger of caisson disease, or "bends."

Camellion was amazed at the lightweight helmet. It was made of some very hard, clear material, possibly polychrome plastic, and did not contain either a mouthpiece or an oral-nasal mask. The air flowed freely from a series of holes in the metal rim to which the helmet was attached.

The dry "constant volume" suit, made of half-inch-thick neoprene, had special provisions to maintain the same volume at different depths, thereby maintaining a constant buoyancy. The suit was heated by a diver heat source using a catalytic magnesium burner. Camellion would be well protected against the icy waters of the Arctic Ocean.

Attached to the Death Merchant's weighted belt were three magnetic mines, each weighing seven pounds and measuring six inches in diameter. One mine could blow a four-foot hole in the side of any submarine.

The Death Merchant pulled one of the electric prods from its clamp on the wall and studied it. Made of lightweight aluminum, the prod was seven feet long and as thick and as rounded as the average flashlight. Toward the center of the shaft, just above the hand-rest grooves, was a large red push-button. Inside the shaft, which was screwed together in the center, were special batteries and a build-up system that—as Dr. Dubanova had explained—provided enough voltage and amperage to electrocute a fish—or a man. One press of the button, and the ends of the metal prods—each end capped by six inches of stainless steel and copper—became electrified.

Yeah. If one prod was good, two had to be better. The Death Merchant pulled another prod-pole from the wall. Then he walked over to the intercom button on the wall and pressed it.

"Doctor, I'm ready to go out and pay a come-to-visit call on Vershensky and Company. What's the other boat doing now?"

"It is still there, Mr. Camellion," Dr. Dubanova's voice floated back. "It is motionless, it's bow pointed toward us. Wait! It is now moving toward us! You had better hurry, Mr. Camellion!"

"Right! I'm as good as gone!" Camellion said. *And as good as dead if I'm not careful!* He switched off the communicator, took another pole-prod from the wall, and put on his flippers, thinking it odd that the Russians would use black flippers for blue diving suits.

Maybe the off-color scheme served as some kind of special underwater identification.

As the British would say, "Let's have a go at it, old chap."

He went to the diving chute in the center of the lock-out chamber. Holding the two prods perpendicularly, he leaped into the dark waters of the five-foot-wide diving well.

No matter how much time a diver spends in the depths of the sea, each time he dives he always has the feeling that he has intruded into another world, a realm of deceptive peace and quiet, a domain wanting and waiting to kill him, to annihilate him, quickly, quietly, and efficiently.

As he swam from underneath the submarine, the Death Merchant had the same strange feeling of intrusion, a feeling he promptly lost when he saw that the other "passenger little-boat" had stopped some forty to forty-five yards away and, like a baby whale giving birth to its young, was discharging divers from its own lock-out chamber—one, two, three, four, five of the pig farmers! Five grim figures in red deep-diving suits and blue flippers.

And each Russkie has an electric prod! Double fudge!

Camellion realized that since the Russians had had no way of knowing his own plans, the five divers were going to do to his boat what he intended to do to theirs—blow his submarine out of the water!

Their legs pounding the water, the five Russians swam toward the Death Merchant, who was far from being a stranger in the water. Richard swam upward, and the five Ivans followed, moving at an angle that would intersect his, should he continue on the same ascending course. The Death Merchant changed tactics. When he and the Russians were only twenty feet apart, he flipped forward and drove straight down, then twisted and shot upward again, his quick, double movements placing him directly beneath two divers who hadn't the time either to anticipate his strategy or to move out of his way. But Camellion was far from safe. Two other divers had dived around and, like two sharks coming in for the kill, were right behind him, closing in fast, their deadly prods extended.

The two Russians above Camellion rolled over in the blue water, both men frantically trying to avoid the Death Merchant and, at the same time, stab him with their prods. Richard, using the pole-prod in his right hand, knocked aside one Russian's prod and arched his body in time to avoid being hit by the other diver, whose mighty thrust propelled him toward Camellion. The end of the Russian's prod missed Camellion by only a few inches, but Camellion made contact. He jabbed outward to the left, pressed the button, and the end of his prod caught one Russian in the back. There was a bright blue flash in the water, a loud sizzling sound, and Boris Frolov went limp, killed instantly by the intense shock.

While Frolov floated limply in the water, his arms and legs outstretched, his head pointed downward, the Death Merchant kicked his legs violently and propelled his body to the right. He then twisted himself and dove downward, his arms and legs moving like the overworked vanes of a windmill. The two divers who had been in back of him tried to follow, diving after him. But Camellion was too fast. Before either Leonty Pogin or Yuri Royko could put together what was happening, Richard executed a wide loop and was coming up behind them. Pogin and Royko parted, each man swimming off violently to one side, their plan being to cut around and catch the Death Merchant in the flanks while Colonel Wrangel and Invid Litex closed in from each end. None of the four Russians were fast enough. Camellion jerked himself out of the path of Wrangel's prod. In response, Wrangel humped over, dove down, twisted around, and began coming up for another try. In the meanwhile, Camellion blocked Litex's prod by thrusting out his own two aluminum staffs and forming them into an X that caught a foot of Litex's prod and pushed it up and out of harm's way. Camellion rolled over on his back and moved downward head-first to avoid Yuri Royko's thrust. At the same instant he stabbed out at Royko with his left prod and upward with the other prod, at Leonty Pogin, who was coming in from the other side. He missed Royko, who swam on by, but his right prod touched Pogin's shoulder. Another blue flash in the water, a sizzling sound, and Leonty Pogin was dead and falling into Deathland.

Now the Death Merchant dove straight up, leveled off, and fishtailed it toward the KGB submarine, the three pig farmers following as fast as they could. They had seen the magnetic mines fastened to the Death Merchant's belt and had correctly deduced his intention. Now they assumed he was going to try to swim all the way to their sub and slap the mines against its hull before they could stop him.

The Death Merchant suddenly surprised them by turning around and swimming straight toward them, his twin prods cutting the water like two silver spears.

Startled and unnerved by Camellion's unexpected turnabout, the three KGB divers parted company, cutting to the left, Litex downward and slightly to the right. The three men didn't swim more than fifteen feet before they turned and came right back at the Death Merchant—a logical maneuver on the part of the Russians, one that should have culminated in Camellion's being electrocuted. The move might have worked if the Death Merchant had played the game according to the rules. But when Yuri Royko was swimming down at him, Camellion kicked himself around and did the unexpected—he used his aluminum prod as a spear, throwing it the short distance at Royko, who tried to get out of its way by rolling sideways in the water. The Russian almost succeeded—almost. But the tip of Camellion's prod caught the Russian in the left ankle. A blue flash! A sizzle! And death claimed another pig farmer by the name of Yuri Royko.

Fear and desperation, especially fear of death, can make fighting fools of even cowards. Colonel Wrangel and Invid Litex, knowing they were fighting for their very lives, tried to close in on the deadly Death Merchant. Wrangel swam in from the left while Litex cut upward through the water.

Camellion again executed an unexpected movement. Instead of swimming upward or knifing his body to the right, he kicked out his legs, turned in the churning

160

water, and swam straight at Colonel Wrangel, whose hatred of Camellion had instilled in him a grim and violent determination to kill this *Amerikanski* who had destroyed Zemlya II. To keep the Death Merchant's own electric prod away from him, Wrangel began using his prod like a broadsword, moving it back and forth in front of him. Because of the resistance of the icy water, he couldn't swish the prod with any great speed but he felt the motion was sufficient to keep the Death Merchant away from him.

The Death Merchant swam straight at Colonel Wrangel, whose rapidly moving prod was churning water on all sides. When it seemed that Wrangel might be in a position to make prod-contact with the Death Merchant, Camellion's left hand shot out and grabbed the KGB officer's prod as the aluminum shaft was cutting through the water toward him, his fingers closing around the metal a foot above the stainless steel tip.

During those few moments, Wrangel was helpless, as defenseless as a newborn baby. He tried to jerk the prod from Camellion's grasp, pulling it violently toward him with both hands. A second later he felt a brief stab of intense agony; then there was nothing, nothing but a velvet blackness as wide as eternity and as deep as infinity.

The tip of the Death Merchant's prod had caught Wrangel in the chest. The KGB colonel was dead. He went limp and began to float with the current, the prod falling slowly from his gloved hands.

Camellion looped his body in time to avoid a prod thrust by Invid Litex, who possessed more than a goodly amount of nerve though he didn't have much sense. He hoped that the Death Merchant would try to rush him, in which case the damned *Amerikanski* would rush straight in and perhaps leave himself exposed.

The Death Merchant did no such thing. He dived straight down, turned again, and shot upward to the rear of Litex, whose nerve deserted him. Litex was suddenly consumed with a terrible fear and a terrible urge to live—if only for a little while longer.

Camellion jabbed straight out with his electric prod, but the Russian didn't kick around to meet the attack.

161

Instead, Litex began fishtailing toward the KGB sub some ten yards away, kicking his legs violently, his flippers thrashing the water like two paddle wheels.

With all the speed of a starving barracuda, Camellion shot after the Russian, who swam underneath the sub in a desperate effort to reach the l.o.c. diving well. Litex succeeded! He was moving up through the chute, his legs still sticking out of the mouth of the well, when the tip of the Death Merchant's prod touched the sole of his right foot. A flash, a sizzle, and Invid Litex jerked and died. He had been electrocuted as neatly as if he had sat in an electric chair. Ordinarily, the body of the Russian would have drifted upward within the rounded well of the chute, but the shock of electrocution had made him push against the metal side of the chute, the movement sending his body backward. The corpse shot downward, floating so close to the Death Merchant that he could observe the horror-stricken face through the helmet. Invid Litex was not a pretty sight. His eyes and mouth were wide open. He looked frozen, which he wasn't. He looked stone dead, which he was.

The Death Merchant went to work. He removed a mine from his weighed belt, pressed the small switch that made the mine magnetic, slapped the bottom against the hull of the sub, and pulled off the activating seal. There was no timer. According to Dr. Dubanova, each mine had previously been set to explode after an interval of twelve minutes. As Camellion swam underneath the boat to the port side, he was acutely aware that time was running out. He couldn't see his wristwatch, but his keen sense of timing quietly informed him that in less than fifteen minutes, Dome 1 and Dome 3 would blow themselves apart.

In less than 900 seconds, Zemlya II would cease to exist!

Chapter Fourteen

People in general don't realize it, but it is not being dead that terrifies them as much as the thought of dying. It's the fear of dying itself which fills their lives with moments of dread. Even less fortunate are those who, though a prank of fate, know when they are going to take the one-way trip to Deathland. Knowing when fills them with a nameless, numbing horror that defies description.

General Vershensky, Major Sedin, and Captain Tur knew the feeling felt by all men about to be executed. They were going to die, and they knew they were going to die. Worse, they knew there wasn't anything they could do to prevent their dying.

The three Russian KGB officers had been forced to watch the underwater battle in the television screen whose camera gave them a view of the bow. As helpless as a turtle on its back, they had seen the Death Merchant kill four of the agents. The last diver had then retreated, the Death Merchant following, the bow TV camera losing the images of both men as they swam underneath the keel of the submarine.

Major Sedin cut the boat's power to zero. An awful silence followed in which Sedin, Tur, and Vershensky waited and listened, stunned beyond helplessness, not knowing what to do. They had been ruthless in life, and the KGB manuals had not instructed them how to die!

"Do you think the Death Merchant got whoever it was?" Captain Tur choked out, looking dumbly at Sedin and Vershensky.

"Shut up and listen!" whispered Vershensky. "If Camellion didn't kill him, he'll be coming forward in a few minutes."

"The Death Merchant might follow," whispered

163

Major Sedin, drawing a Stechkin machine pistol from its holster. "I don't think he will. I think he—"

"I said shut up and listen!" rasped Vershensky, cocking his head to one side.

The three Russians waited as if deaf and dumb, none of them moving. They almost jumped when they heard the slight clang against the side of the vessel. There was no way they could pretend the ominous sound was other than what it was: metal coming into contact with metal, the slapping of a magnetic mine against the hull of the underseas U-boat, a signal that the life stock of the three KGB officers had fallen by a hundred points.

"He's planted a mine!" Captain Tur said huskily, his voice trembling slightly. "Damn it, there must be something we can do! We can't just let him blow us out of the ocean!"

"There were only six diving suits back there," Major Sedin said tonelessly, "and the sixth suit doesn't have any air bottles. Even if one of us could go outside, what good would it do? Let's be honest about the situation. None of us are a match for the Death Merchant!"

"That's deviationist talk, Comrade," Vershensky said stiffly. He thrust out his bulldog of a chin. "The center would not like it!"

"It's the truth, Comrade General," Major Sedin said, sticking to his guns. "And you know it."

Before a surprised General Vershensky could reply, there was another clanking sound from the other side of the submarine.

"He's put another mine on us!" Captain Tur said hollowly. Silver beads of sweat stood out on his grimy face, and his left eyelid started to twitch.

General Vershensky sat down in the bucket seat and let his body slump. "We have only one chance." He spoke in a low voice, and the other two Russians got the impression that their chief was already resigned to death. "We will return to Zemlya II. If we can reach the dock area, we may be able to get out of the boat before the mines explode. We will then have a chance to reach the diving chamber igloo in Dome 1. If we succeed, we'll live."

No sooner had Vershensky stopped speaking than

Major Sedin pressed the power button, and again a loud humming filled the sub. He was about ready to turn the boat to starboard and guide it back to the doomed underwater city when he and the other two men heard a loud tapping from the forward section of the U-boat.

The three KGB officials glanced nervously at each other. The tapping had to come from the Death Merchant, but what was he up to? They stared then into the bow TV screen and saw him. There he was, his feet treading water as he kept his body in front of the bow TV camera. He held a mine in one hand and was actually thumbing his nose at them with the other.

The damned Death Merchant was actually mocking them!

Captain Tur's lower jaw fell. Major Sedin inhaled fearfully.

"That son of a bitch!" screamed General Vershensky in a rage. Hell is too good a place for such an impudent swine!"

"He has the nerve of a devil!" Major Sedin said in an awed voice.

He and the other two KGB officers stared at the screen, cursing Camellion as he pointed to the mine and slapped it down on the hull to one side of the camera housing.

Just as unexpectedly, more figures appeared on the screen!

"Comrades—look!" shouted Tur, pointing at the bow screen. "There behind the Death Merchant—other divers. Do you see them, Comrades?"

"Yes, more than a dozen, but it is difficult to tell their number in the dark water!" Major Sedin said excitedly. "They have to be from our nuclear sub. There is no other logical answer."

Very suddenly, the three Russians found it difficult to believe what their eyes told them to be true. Coming down at the red-suited divers was another group of men clad in white suits!

"This doesn't make sense!" gasped Captain Tur. "Who are the other divers? Where have they come from?"

"Idiots! There has to be an *Amerikanski* submarine in the area!" spit out General Vershensky, gripping the edge of the bucket seat. "No doubt the same submarine which carried Camellion on his mission. Sedin, get us out of here and back to the dock at Zemlya. There is nothing we can do but try to save our lives! Hurry!"

After planting the third and last mine on the bow of the sub and swimming off to one side, Richard Camellion was shocked when he spotted the red-suited divers fifty yards to his rear. A man who never underestimated or overestimated any situation, he felt he was as good as dead. In those few seconds, he counted fourteen divers, each one armed with what appeared to be a spear-gun. They'd kill him in several minutes.

Camellion's pragmatic acceptance of death was abruptly changed to a hope for life by what he saw next: another group of divers, these in white deep-diving suits, knifing down through the water to cut off the Russians. Richard at once figured out what had to be the only correct answer: the pig farmers were from the Russian nuclear submarine. The other divers had to be from an American U-boat.

Albacore? Impossible! In this business there were no miracles!

The Russian divers should have stayed home! Within a quarter of a minute, both Russian and American divers had met and were fighting, white streaks crisscrossing up and down and back and forth in the water as both groups fired spear-guns. The Americans, however, were better fighters and better swimmers. Although three Americans died with steel spears protruding from their bodies, in just as short a time, seven Russians died. Two more Russians went bye bye to Deathland during the Russians' retreat. The last the Death Merchant saw of the five Russians they were fishtailing through the water, swimming away from the area, no doubt headed back to their submarine. Very quickly they had disappeared in the dark water.

And here I am, all dressed up in a pig farmer swimsuit, Camellion told himself. He watched the white-suited divers swim toward him, let the electric prod slip from his hand, and began swimming toward them. Twenty feet from the first two divers, who kept their spear guns pointed in his direction, Camellion stopped swimming, kicked himself into a perpendicular position, and put his arms above his head, treading water to keep himself stationary.

The divers closed in around the Death Merchant, dangling in a ring, hemming him in. As close as they were, Camellion could see the square American flags and *U.S.S. Albacore* printed on their chests.

One of the divers moved in close and inspected Camellion. But the Death Merchant could not see the man's face behind the gogglelike mask of his deep-diving suit. The man put out his hand and began tapping on the Death Merchant's helmet with one finger.

Identify yourself! he tapped out in Morse code.

The Death Merchant reached out with his own hand and, with one finger, tapped a reply against the face plate of the other diver.

I'm Camellion. Saddle-Soap: Two Bars, *or hasn't Commander Stacher or any of his execs given you the code key to the mission?*

No. But if you know our bearded skipper, you must be the Death Merchant.

Camellion smiled and tapped back, *Quit conning me, sailor. Stacher wouldn't be caught dead with a beard, and you know it. Let's can the small talk. We have to get to the other Russian sub. Dr. Dubanova, the reason for my mission, is waiting in that sub."*

The Death Merchant pointed to the "little-boat," which was only a short distance away.

The *Albacore* diver nodded and tapped out: *Okay, Camellion. We'll go get her. She can put on a suit, if there's another one in the sub, and she can swim back to the* Albacore *with us.*

How far away is the Albacore?

About a mile. We're resting on the bottom behind a ridge. That's why the Russian's big sub didn't spot us, and the Gf mechanism helped. And we don't have to worry about the Russian sub. We sneaked up behind her and fouled up her screws with a steel net. It will take the Russians several hours to free her. By then we'll be out of the area."

We don't have time to get Dubanova and swim to the Albacore! Camellion tapped frantically. *We don't even have time to swim to the* Albacore *if we don't go after* Dubanova. *About five tons of nitrostarch is about to go bang in the Russian underwater base, and if we're caught out here, the shock waves will bat us around like ping-pong balls at the bottom of Niagara Falls. Our only chance is to get inside that midget sub, and we'd better get there damn fast!*

Why in hell didn't you say so! Let's move it!

The diver from *Albacore* raised his arm and pointed to the odd-looking "little-boat", telling the other American divers that it was their immediate destination.

Still dressed in their deep-diving suits, but minus their headgear, flippers, and back air tanks, Camellion and Lieutenant Wallow, the leader of the *Albacore* frogmen, stood in the control compartment, watching the TV screens with Dr. Dubanova. The compartment was very hot because, for some obscure reason, the air-conditioning system had quit functioning.

The Death Merchant looked at his wristwatch. "Either I'm fast, or the timers back at Zemlya II are slow." He glanced at Dr. Dubanova, "I hope you assembled them properly, Doctor."

"I'm am an electrical engineer, Mr. Camellion!" Dr. Dubanova said haughtily. "To make a simple electrical timer is child's play! The explosives will detonate. You will both see!"

In the TV screen whose camera monitored the stern they could see Zemlya II, the five domes barely visible in the water, each dome seeming not more than a foot in diameter. They could even see the "Sea Spider" underwater weather station, with its four steel legs, its twenty-foot aluminum float appearing to be no larger than a marble.

Camellion and company saw something else in the distance: General Vershensky's submarine, the tiny U-boat appearing to be no more than several inches long in the clear Arctic water. The midget sub was moving at full speed toward the mouth of the tube which would take the vehicle to the dock lock-out chamber in Dome 1. The sub slowed speed and was about to enter the tube when the three mines attached to her hull exploded

—so suddenly that Dr. Dubanova drew back in alarm and put one hand over her mouth.

Camellion and his two companions heard three dull *woommmsssss,* the sounds coming so close together they sounded almost like one explosion. There was a lot of agitated water where the sub had been, followed by jagged parts of metal tumbling away from each other in irregular motions. Quickly the embroilment quieted down and there was nothing, nothing but a strange emptiness, except for a few drifting parts of wreckage.

"Scratch one KGB general, right Camellion?" Lieutenant Wallow mused. A freckled-faced man in his early thirties, he put a hand on the Death Merchant's shoulder.

"Hopefully, General Vershensky's top aides were with him on the sub," the Death Merchant said, his eyes not leaving the television screens above the control panel.

The Arctic Ocean, by almost twenty seconds, preceded the blasts in Dome 1 and Dome 2. The trigger might have been the crack in Dome 2, the one caused by Camellion's demolishing the lock-door with rocket shells. The crack might have finally admitted defeat to the constant, insistent pressure of the water and have collapsed. No one would ever know. All Camellion and Wallow and Dubanova saw was one side of the dome buckle slowly inward, the way one side of a balloon sags from a slow leak. A few moments later, the ocean began to pour into the dome, the raging waters crushing the blue igloos, the tremendous wall of waves rolling toward the armory where the timers on the bars of nitrostarch clicked off the last and final second.

With a sound resembling deep and distant thunder, the armory exploded. There was a gigantic flash on the television screen. The water was excited with the kind of force and violence that usually comes from the eruption of an undersea volcano, a seething turbulence of pure destruction before which even the Death Merchant felt insignificant and humbled.

The ocean was still convulsing angrily when there was another smothered roar and another brief outburst of blow-up from the nitrostarch exploding in the sub-shuttle car Camellion had parked in the control dome.

The Death Merchant, hanging onto a hand-hold on the wall, leaned down and flipped the switch of the communicator, which would pipe his voice throughout the boat to the *Albacore* frogmen in other compartments of the submarine.

"Brace yourselves for shock waves!" he yelled. All the while he kept his eyes on the television screen.

Due to the second explosion, the ocean again raged as if touched by an invisible tornado, the sheer vehemence of the maelstrom sending tiny shivers of fear flowing through Dr. Dubanova and Lieutenant Wallow.

Suddenly the submarine was rocked back and forth like a giant swing from port to starboard, the waves of shock rocking the boat on its beam, forcing the bow to rise and dip sharply with the churning of the water.

Slowly the water quieted down. The submarine returned to normal buoyancy, and the television screens cleared.

Of Zemlya II there was no trace, the shroud of the Arctic Ocean covering the area where the five domes had been; and all that remained to mark the former location of the Russian city under the sea were two crooked legs of the "Sea Spider" weather station—two skinny tombstones that looked oddly out of place.

Zemlya II had been utterly destroyed.

"I wonder if Dr. Borsilinskow and the other scientists managed to escape to the surface in the safety chambers?" Dr. Dubanova asked in a sad voice, her English clipped and precise.

"I doubt if anything could have lived through those blasts," Lieutenant Wallow said matter of factly.

The Death Merchant did not make any kind of comment. He had Raya Dubanova. She had the secret, and that's all that mattered.

Saddle-Soap: Two Bars had been completed.

The most dangerous mission he had ever undertaken was a success.

Addendum

The Death Merchant, dressed in a pair of starched blue coveralls and sitting on the bunk in one of the officer compartments, fingered the folded piece of paper, the message from the radio room a sailor had just brought to him. At the moment he wasn't in the mood to receive any kind of news, be it good or bad. His thoughts were still fixed on the deadly details Dr. Dubanova had confided to him.

Quite by accident, during their research involving various projects, Dr. Dubanova, Dr. Borsilinskow, and Dr. Krasnoyarsk had discovered that world civilization was about to come to a sudden, violent, and inglorious end, within the next twenty years.

"I realize the implication of what I am saying," Dr. Dubanova had said, once she and Camellion were safely aboard the *Albacore* and the nuclear submarine was leaving the area. "For almost three years we worked to obtain proof. Six months ago, we found this mathematical proof, which your own scientists will confirm. Mathematics is an exact science, as I'm sure you know."

Dr. Dubanova had explained that since the Soviet Government would not have believed its top scientists—the men in the Kremlin had a peasant mentality and were only interested in world expansion of Communism —she and the other scientists had decided to reveal the secret of the coming catastrophe to the United States Government. US authorities, in government and in scientific circles, could then prepare the peoples of the world for the final doom.

Camellion sighed. How deluded could one be? Poor Dr. Dubanova and her colleagues, to assume that US scientists would announce the end of the world! Mathematical confirmation would not make a bit of difference. The US Government would not announce one single word about the coming destruction. It would not because it could not. Who would believe any announcement that the world was coming to the end? Even if US spokesmen were believed, why create world panic? What good would it do? Panic wouldn't be able to stop the coming cataclysm.

The theory alone was too horrible to be believed, at least by "God-fearin' folk" who, to preserve their sanity, had to believe that man and his works would endure forever.

The cause of the cataclysm? The earth would again (Dr. Dubanova had said "again!") shift its sixty-mile-thick shell. The poles would move almost to the equator in a fraction of a day. Again the atmosphere and oceans, refusing to change directions with Earth's shell, would wipe out most life. What would be left of humanity would slowly begin to rebuild and reinvent.

Why? The Death Merchant thought of Doctor Dubanova's explanation. If you could view Earth in cross-section, you would see two molten layers and a central core. The important thing is the thin molten layer about sixty miles thick which lies between sixty and 120 miles below the surface of the earth. The dynamic balance of the shell of the Earth as it is today seems precarious. The Death Merchant had already known that on a summer weekend, traffic moving north between New York City and Albany on Friday night shifted the Earth's shell, displacing the South Pole a few feet; when the travelers went south, back to New York on Sunday evening, the shift reversed and the South Pole would slide back into place. He knew this was not some kind of fiction. Scientists had measured the shift.

In general calculations, the imbalance of Earth's shell shows a torque—a turning or twisting force—of some 48.6 by 10^{15}-ton miles, enough to shift the shell with the equatorial pivot points being near 0° and 180° longitude. If this force were active the Bay of Bengal would end up at the North Pole; the Pacific west of Peru would end up at the South Pole.

"Yet despite this torque the shell of the Earth is not shifting," Dr. Dubanova had said. "This means that

172

somewhere there must be an equal and opposite torque. What is it?"

The Russians had discovered the answer, which lay in the molten layers under the Earth's solid shell. If the shift were to occur, the shallow molten layer that is from sixty to 120 miles deep would have to serve as the lubricant for the shift. When no shift occurs, the torque opposing the shift has to come from within this layer.

"The Hannes Alfvens experiments with mercury, which demonstrate the extraordinary effects produced by combining magnetic and electric energy into magnetohydrodynamic, or MHD, energy, show what is happening within the molten layer," Dr. Dubanova had explained. "It is known there are both electric currents and magnetic fields inside Earth. Combined, their MHD energy structure makes the molten layers act as if they were near solid, or plastic. Seismology indicates extremely low shear strength.

"Our paleomagnetic studies indicate that many times in the past our planet has gone through magnetic reversals. These reversals are caused by magnetic zones, between which 'nulls' exist, are galactic-scale concentric spheres, with the 'nulls' containing asteroid belts. The entire solar system is moving outward in our Milky Way galaxy, and in so going travels from one magnetic zone to the next. In the 'null' zones, between the two magnetic zones, the MHD structure within Earth is weakened to the extent that it no longer can supply the equal and opposite torque which prevents Earth's shell from shifting to a new balance. The shell's torque takes over completely and Earth's shell shifts to a new position in a fraction of one day. The ice caps wind up rotating equatorially, melting in tropical heat, and new ice caps begin to form at the new poles. Think of what this means, Mr. Camellion! It means that ice ages are not a matter of advancing ice caps, but are a matter of relocation of the Earth's outer shell."

The Death Merchant had not argued with Dr. Dubanova. He was not a scientist.

"We must face the fact that a worldwide flood is a very normal part of Earth's life cycle," she had said.

"It reshuffles all of its natural resources and gives the human race a chance to start over again. It revitalizes the species! Can you conceive of Moscow believing any of this? Nonetheless, it is true. We estimate that such a cataclysm has happened about 300 times in the past history of the planet and will occur about 300 more times before our solar system enters the deep sleep before being reborn."

"And you and your people are positive that the next catastrophe is only a few years away?" Camellion had said.

Doctor Dubanova had nodded solemnly. "Signs indicate the Earth is rapidly approaching a magnetic null zone. We couldn't mathematically pinpoint the exact time, but we're certain that the shift will occur within the next fifteen years. We are positive, and your American scientists will be, too, once we present our equations to them."

The Death Merchant, leaning back on the bunk, thought of the worldwide destruction that would occur during the next cataclysm. There would be no warning. The low rumble would grow into a tremendous roar. Mountains would shake over the entire earth, and the oceans would rear back, piling up into mountains of water more than three miles high; then these mountains of water would rush forward, aided by winds that would blow with the force of a hundred tornadoes.

The Pacific Ocean would move eastward over the United States, burying cities under walls of water and mud. Every building would be smashed; every living thing torn apart, blown or washed across the tortured countryside. Nothing would be able to stop the tremendous onslaught of wind and water as they raced across the North American continent.

Central and South American would suffer the same fate. Within a matter of hours Peru, Ecuador, and western Brazil would be ripped apart by the devastating earthquake, scorched by fire that would break through the surface of the earth, and buried under miles of Pacific Ocean.

Europe, too, would die as the terrible Atlantic would

174

pile higher and higher, following the howling winds eastward. The Alps, the Urals, the Pyrenees, and the Scandinavian mountains would be heaved even higher into the sky before the miles-high walls of water struck.

If the Russian calculations were correct—and the Death Merchant had no doubt that they were—the Sahara Desert and West Africa would simply disappear under the raging attack of wind and water. But the area bounded by the Congo, South Africa, and Kenya would suffer only severe winds and earthquakes. Survivors, however, would marvel at the sun's standing stationary in the sky for almost half a day, bringing to the minds of some observers that day described in the Old Testament when the sun stood still.

As the Arctic basin left is polar home, eastern Siberia, Manchuria, China, and Burma would be subjected to the same elements as the rest of the earth: wind, earth-fire, flooding, then freezing. The cold would be incredible. Everything would freeze—men, beasts, plants, and mud all would be stone-hard within a matter of hours. The torn bodies of men and animals would be piled into gigantic mountains of flesh and bone, buried under tons of mud and seawater and fianlly set by the terrible paralyzing cold.

The wind and water would howl and rage for six days and six nights. During the sixth day the oceans would begin to settle in their new beds, to run off the high places. On the seventh day, the hideous rampage would end.

The Arctic Ice Age would be over and done with, and a new Stone Age would begin.

There would be other physical changes. The Bay of Bengal, now directly east of India, would now be the new North Pole. Just west of Peru, in the Pacific Ocean, would be the new South Pole. The present ice caps of Greenland and Antarctica would rotate equatorially in the new Torrid Zone. The ice caps would dissolve in the tropical heat, and the tremendous walls of water thus released would surge toward the newly created oceans, taking everything in their path and creating immense seasonal moraines. In less than fifty years, the ice caps would melt, and the world's oceans would rise by 225 feet. For generations the new Torrid Zone would be shrouded in fog from the enormous amounts of moisture poured into the atmosphere by the melting ice caps.

New ice caps would begin to form in the new polar areas. In Greenland and Antarctica verdant tropical foliage would sprout.

Camellion's face was solemn. There was more than enough evidence that Earth had suffered previous floods. For example, the Alaskan muck packed with animal bones and debris, thousands of tons of the stuff—mastodon, mammoth, horses, bison, bears, and even lions, camels, and other tropical animals. A faunal population that came to a sudden end in the middle of some cataclysmic catastrophe—and was frozen very suddenly. How could tropical animals be found in Alaska, unless they had been carried there by mountain-high waves?

The Death Merchant thought of other evidence. The Beresovka mammoth, found in Siberia, frozen in mud, buttercups still in its mouth! The Piri Reis map, showing the North Pole in the Sudan Basin! The computable age of the Antarctic and Greenland ice caps, at about 6,500 years! The legends from primitive man in Tierra del Fuego at the southern tip of South America of the day the sun set in the wrong direction! The legends from Malayan and Sumatran aborigines of the long night! The correlation of ice ages and quick extinctions the world over! The fantastic evidence of a burgeoning tropical population in Alaska and in parts of Siberia, all of it completely wiped out very suddenly. The astonishing find of a coral reef on the floor of the Arctic Ocean! And much evidence, enough to fill a large book!

Camellion rose from the bunk, went over to a metal desk jutting out from the wall, and sat down. He was positive of one thing—if and when the deluge happened, the pitiful survivors of the human race would have an Adam and Eve story all over again, similar to the one of 11,500 years ago, and a Noah story like that of 6,500 years ago.

As Dr. Dubanova had said in a low, strained voice, "The survivors will be driven into another Stone Age like the old Stone Age of 11,500 years ago, and the New Stone Age of 6,500 years ago which followed the last two inundations. As surely as night follows day, as surely as man is just beginning to scratch the surface of learning since the last two cataclysms, the next flooding will come within fifteen years."

If she's right, Camellion thought, *after this tumble we'll join Noah, Adam and Eve, Mu, Atlantis, and Olympus—and Jesus Christ will join Osiris, Zeus, Vishnu, and the other gods.*

But despite end-of-the-world hell and catastrophic high water, the Death Merchant didn't lose sight of the fact that he had a job to do. He unfolded the piece of paper and stared at the single word.

Algeria.

Damn it! Richard hated Algeria. He despised all of northern Africa. Any mission in Algeria would have to be a nightmare.

He had torn up the paper and was throwing the pieces in the wastebasket when he remembered something else Dr. Dubanova had said: "Such world-wide catastrophes were known to the ancients, and I am not referring to the Biblical Flood."

"That story was taken from the Babylonian Epic of Gilgamesh," Camellion had told her. "The Gilgamesh tale is the primeval version of Noah's flood, written thousands of years before the Hebrews wrote the version we find in Genesis."

"I was thinking of something else in the Bible," Dr. Dubanova said in a quiet voice. "From Psalms 46: 2-3. 'Therefore will not we fear, though the earth be removed, and though the mountains be carried into the midst of the sea;

" 'Though the waters thereof roar and be troubled, though the mountains shake with the swelling thereof.' "

PINNACLE BOOKS

THE INCREDIBLE ACTION PACKED SERIES

DEATH MERCHANT

by Joseph Rosenberger

His name is Richard Camellion, he's a master of disguise, deception and destruction. He does what the CIA and FBI cannot do. They call him THE DEATH MERCHANT!

Order		Title	Book #	Price
_____	# 1	THE DEATH MERCHANT	P211	.95¢
_____	# 2	OPERATION OVERKILL	P245	.95¢
_____	# 3	THE PSYCHOTRON PLOT	P117	.95¢
_____	# 4	CHINESE CONSPIRACY	P168	.95¢
_____	# 5	SATAN STRIKE	P182	.95¢
_____	# 6	ALBANIAN CONNECTION	P670	$1.25
_____	# 7	CASTRO FILE	P264	.95¢
_____	# 8	BILLIONAIRE MISSION	P339	.95¢
_____	# 9	THE LASER WAR	P399	.95¢
_____	#10	THE MAINLINE PLOT	P473	$1.25
_____	#11	MANHATTAN WIPEOUT	P561	$1.25
_____	#12	THE KGB FRAME	P642	$1.25
_____	#13	THE MATO GROSSO HORROR	P705	$1.25

TO ORDER

Please check the space next to the book/s you want, send this order form together with your check or money order, include the price of the book/s and 25¢ for handling and mailing, to:

PINNACLE BOOKS, INC. / P.O. Box 4347
Grand Central Station/New York, N.Y. 10017

☐ CHECK HERE IF YOU WANT A FREE CATALOG.

I have enclosed $_____ check_____ or money order_____ as payment in full. No C.O.D.'s.

Name_____

Address_____

City_____ State_____ Zip_____
(Please allow time for delivery.)

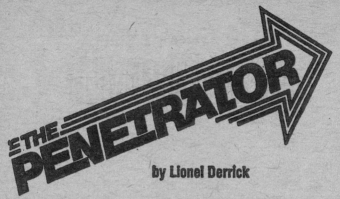

IT'S ALWAYS ACTION WITH

BLADE

HEROIC FANTASY SERIES
by Jeffrey Lord

The continuing saga of a modern man's exploits in the hitherto uncharted realm of worlds beyond our knowledge. Richard Blade is everyman and at the same time, a mighty and intrepid warrior. In the best tradition of America's most popular fictional heroes—giants such as Tarzan, Doc Savage and Conan—

Order		Title	Book No.	Price
_____	# 1	THE BRONZE AXE	P201	$ .95
_____	# 2	THE JADE WARRIOR	P202	$ .95
_____	# 3	JEWEL OF THARN	P203	$ .95
_____	# 4	SLAVE OF SARMA	P204	$ .95
_____	# 5	LIBERATOR OF JEDD	P205	$ .95
_____	# 6	MONSTER OF THE MAZE	P206	$ .95
_____	# 7	PEARL OF PATMOS	P767	$1.25
_____	# 8	UNDYING WORLD	P208	$ .95
_____	# 9	KINGDOM OF ROYTH	P295	$ .95
_____	#10	ICE DRAGON	P768	$1.25
_____	#11	DIMENSION OF DREAMS	P474	$1.25
_____	#12	KING OF ZUNGA	P523	$1.25
_____	#13	THE GOLDEN STEED	P559	$1.25
_____	#14	THE TEMPLES OF AYOCAN	P623	$1.25
_____	#15	THE TOWERS OF MELNON	P688	$1.25

AND MORE TO COME . . .

TO ORDER

Please check the space next to the book/s you want, send this order form together with your check or money order, include the price of the book/s and 25¢ for handling and mailing, to:

PINNACLE BOOKS, INC.

P.O. Box 4347/Grand Central Station/New York, N.Y. 10017

☐ CHECK HERE IF YOU WANT A FREE CATALOG.

I have enclosed $_____check_____or money order_____
as payment in full. No C.O.D.s.

Name_____

Address_____

City_____State_____Zip_____
(Please allow time for delivery.)